PRAISE FOR

“Thrilling and moving i

“Bronsky excels in relat … ses to acknowledge it . . . ins … ng.” *Financial Times*

“Hilarious, disturbing, and … irreverent.” *Kirkus Reviews*

“A Russian doll of a novel, the hidden story of a difficult marriage slowly revealed through the stages of a husband’s care for his terminally ill wife. This is a wise, carefully constructed novel about fragile hidden identities, whose ending reads like a deeply felt beginning.” Elena Lappin, *The Washington Post*

“*Barbara Isn’t Dying* is another short yet substantial novel from Alina Bronsky. Deftly translated by Tim Mohr, the book has echoes with two of the Russian-born German author’s recent works which feature aging protagonists . . . warm, poignant and acerbically funny . . . a sharp-eyed and unsentimental character study of one man and his blinkered view of the world around him.” Malcolm Forbes, *Star Tribune*

“Bronsky’s picture of Walter resonates as deeply poignant, ultimately leaving the reader with a profound sympathy and resigned acceptance of life’s challenges, the process of aging, and ultimately the creation of a new way of life.” Frank Valish, *Under the Radar*

“A remarkably endearing story of a man who realizes he’s taken his loved ones for granted, finds the flaws in his worldview, and works, in this last stage of his life, to change.” *Bustle*, “22 Beach Reads to Bring on Vacation This Summer”

“A wise, carefully constructed novel about fragile hidden identities.” *The Washington Post*

“Skirting sentimentality, and sprinkling what could be a sad tale with plenty of welcome humour, Bronsky makes us root for her unlikely hero.” *Booklist*

“In this tragicomic tale, Herr Schmidt wakes one morning to discover nobody has made the coffee yet—and his immediate thought must be that his wife has died in the night, because what other explanation could there be? Bronsky covers a lot of emotional ground in just 182 pages; I recommend Fredrik Backman fans take a look.” Anne Bogel, *Modern Mrs. Darcy Book Club*

“Cheerful, clever, and full of compassion.” *WDR 3 Mosaic*

"Brimming with dark wit and great warmth." *Sound & Media*

"Bronsky's delicate detachment, her sense of comedy, her feeling for the weird and absurd, make *Barbara Isn't Dying* a delight." *WDR 5*

"The humour is biting, the characters idiosyncratic, the laughter spontaneous—readers will love this new book by Bronsky both for its unsympathetic antihero and for how connected they ultimately feel to him." *emotion*

PRAISE FOR ALINA BRONSKY

"Bronsky has a Dickensian flair for writing about miserable children—or, rather, the miseries of childhood." *Vulture*

"Alina Bronsky brilliantly keeps the mood funny and uplifting throughout with quirky characters and irreverent humour. *My Grandmother's Braid* celebrates the power of forgiveness and the strength of the human spirit." *Apple Books*, Book of the Month

"[Alina Bronsky] is at her best when evoking family dysfunction and powerful, mean old women, and both aspects are promised here [. . .] Sounds like a riot, as ever." *Lit Hub*, Most Anticipated Books of 2021

"*My Grandmother's Braid* is written in a style that seems at turns facetious and tragic; one finds themselves snorting with laughter during the most inappropriate moments [. . .] This book is funny, maddening, and surprisingly sentimental and compassionate. It seems incredible to flip through the one hundred and fifty or so pages that comprise this novel and realize how much there is still to talk about." Barbara Halla, *Asymptote*

"Bronsky's comic take on grandmother makes way for empathy [. . .] Bronsky depicts challenges the ragtag band of characters is up against through gritty city scenes and no-bones-about-it biases. The world of this novel is small, but densely packed with humorous pathos." *Mari's Book Reviews*

"A marvellous tragicomedy told with such lightness as if the author were hovering a few inches above the ground." *Sächsische Zeitung*

"Bronsky is not only a master of the unwritten, but also a magician of perspective and, most importantly, of empathy towards her characters." *Die Tageszeitung*

"Alina Bronsky has written a little masterpiece. Filled with dark humour, at times cynical, *My Grandmother's Braid* is an extraordinarily readable novel, rich in dialogue, and extremely entertaining." *Gießener Allgemeine*

Alina Bronsky is the author of *Broken Glass Park* (Europa, 2010); *The Hottest Dishes of the Tartar Cuisine* (Europa, 2011), named a Best Book of 2011 by *The Wall Street Journal*, *The Huffington Post*, and *Publishers Weekly; Just Call Me Superhero* (Europa, 2014); *Baba Dunja's Last Love* (Europa, 2016); and *My Grandmother's Braid* (Europa, 2021). Born in Yekaterinburg, an industrial town at the foot of the Ural Mountains in central Russia, Bronsky lives in Berlin.

Tim Mohr was an award-winning translator. He also collaborated on memoirs by musicians Gil Scott-Heron, Duff McKagan of Guns N' Roses, and Paul Stanley of KISS. He was the author of *Burning Down the Haus*, a history of political struggle and punk music in East Germany. Prior to starting his writing career, he earned his living as a club DJ in Berlin.

ALSO BY

ALINA BRONSKY

Broken Glass Park

The Hottest Dishes of the Tartar Cuisine

Just Call Me Superhero

Baba Dunja's Last Love

My Grandmother's Braid

Alina Bronsky

BARBARA ISN'T DYING

Translated from the German
by Tim Mohr

Europa
editions

Europa Editions
8 Blackstock Mews
London N4 2BT
www.europaeditions.co.uk

This book is a work of fiction. Any references to historical events, real people, or real locales are used fictitiously.

First publication 2025 by Europa Editions

Translation by Tim Mohr
Original title: *Barbara stirbt nicht*

A catalogue record for this title is available from the British Library
ISBN 978-1-78770-581-4

Bronsky, Alina
Barbara Isn't Dying

Cover design by Ginevra Rapisardi

Cover illustration © Rüdiger Trebels

Prepress by Grafica Punto Print – Rome

The authorized representative in the EEA is Edizioni e/o, via Gabriele Camozzi 1, 00192 Rome, Italy.

Printed and bound in Great Britain by Clays Ltd, Elcograf S.p.A

BARBARA ISN'T DYING

When Herr Schmidt woke up early Friday and didn't smell coffee, at first he thought Barbara might have died in her sleep. It was an absurd idea—Barbara was as healthy as a horse—though even more absurd was the possibility that she could have overslept. She never overslept. But when he turned over in bed and saw that the other half of the bed was empty, it seemed to him that the most likely explanation was that Barbara had keeled over dead on her way to the kitchen.

Herr Schmidt sat up and shoved his feet into his slippers. His nostrils flared longingly, missing the familiar aroma. Whatever happened to Barbara: if she had managed to put on the coffee beforehand, the scent would have wafted upstairs and reached the bedroom. Aromas can't be contained. Herr Schmidt headed off, hoping his wife hadn't fallen down the steps. Though presumably the noise would have awoken him. Or perhaps not: Barbara was a quiet woman, always had been.

He didn't get far. An unfamiliar obstruction loomed before the half-open bathroom door. Herr Schmidt drew closer, recognized Barbara's foot, and then the rest of her. She lay on the tile, looking at him out of one eye while the other slowly, and not completely, opened.

"Walter," she said. "Give me your hand."

Herr Schmidt leaned over her and tried to pull her up. Barbara groaned and pushed him away, which, given the demand to help her, seemed truly illogical. She turned onto her side, braced herself with her hands, and fought despairingly against gravity. Herr Schmidt grabbed her by her armpits and lifted her up. He threw one of her arms around his neck, walked her slowly back toward the bed step by step, and then hoisted her surprisingly heavy body onto the mattress. Her feet were still in her felt slippers, he removed them and placed them one next to the other on the bedside carpet.

"The coffee," Barbara whispered.

"It's fine," said Herr Schmidt. "I don't need it right this second."

"But I do," said Barbara.

This was surprising. Herr Schmidt went slowly down the stairs and looked around the kitchen. This was Barbara's realm, the surfaces gleamed at him. For their golden anniversary he'd given her a kitchen renovation, a collective gift to make up for all the anniversaries and birthdays when he hadn't given her anything, and for all the future ones when he also wouldn't give her anything. The coffee machine stood next to the stove, the plug was removed from the wall for the dual purposes of safety and energy conservation.

Herr Schmidt plugged it back in. He tentatively opened a cabinet, and then the next one. He had never made coffee, something his daughter Karin and her best friend Mai laughed about during their visits.

"Papa, you really don't know where the coffee is?"

"I don't meddle in Barbara's business just as she doesn't meddle in mine."

"And if she isn't here? Or can't do it?"

"Why wouldn't she be here?"

"You can't be serious, Papa. You don't even know where the milk is."

This, of course, was a ridiculous accusation. He knew milk belonged in the fridge, even if the bleached white garbage sold as milk these days could sit out in the sun for weeks without going bad. Real milk belonged in the fridge.

Herr Schmidt opened all the cabinets and then sat back down, looking from his chair at the cabinet on the left and then the one on the right: rice, oats, cream of wheat, polenta, what the hell was all of this stuff?

His next idea was to call Karin and ask her how to make coffee. As a woman she had to know that sort of thing. On the other hand, she would immediately suspect something was wrong. She'd ask questions and make a fuss. This in turn would displease Barbara, who surely didn't want any excitement. Herr Schmidt closed his eyes, demoralized by his thirst for coffee.

Coffee was always ready when he entered the kitchen in the morning. The table was made, two plates, butter, a basket of rolls. He would sit down, Barbara would pour him a cup and add just the right amount of milk. He didn't even know the exact ratio. When they went out to dinner, which they actually never did, she also put the cream in for him.

His gaze landed on the shelf of cookbooks. There were too many, nobody could possibly need all of them. German cuisine, another on German cuisine, French, Italian, vegetarian, baking with love, baking for Christmas, advanced breadmaking. Herr Schmidt leafed through a couple of them, no help at all.

Suddenly he had an inspired idea. The can of coffee jumped into his field of vision, he'd seen it a thousand times without realizing it. The coffee filters were right next to the can. Herr Schmidt put a filter in the plastic housing, filled it to the rim with the blackish-brown grounds, realized that finished coffee was water-based, carried the machine to the faucet, and tilted it slightly: some of the ground coffee spilled out. Once the rear reservoir portion of the machine had filled with water, Herr Schmidt put the device back on the counter and turned it on. The resulting gurgle assured him he'd succeeded.

He trudged upstairs step by step to look in on Barbara.

It wasn't her style to lie around on the bathroom floor in the morning, but she didn't say anything more about it and kept her eyes closed. One needn't discuss everything.

In the kitchen, the clear coffee pot was already half-full of oily, black liquid. Herr Schmidt tasted it and spat it out. He thinned the brew with tap water and added milk. His thirst was too strong, he drank the cup in one go, ignoring the initial hints of heartburn. Barbara, though, was picky when it came to food and drink, he couldn't serve her swill like this.

He drained a second cup and thought it over.

Grocery shopping was Barbara's thing, though sometimes she gave him a short shopping list if he was going to be out with the dog anyway. Usually he just had to pick up four bread rolls, two pretzel rolls, two poppy rolls, and two whole grain rolls at the bakery. That was a week's worth, which Barbara froze and then defrosted day by day for breakfast. The bakery smelled of coffee at all times of the day, and in the corner of the shop a coffee machine wheezed. Herr Schmidt had always wondered what poor souls bought coffee there.

He headed off without Helmut, despite how much he wagged his tail and panted. Through the glazed glass door, Helmut's reproachful look followed Herr Schmidt to the next street corner. Without the dog it took less than the usual eleven minutes to the bakery.

The bakery charged an outrageous 2 euros 80 for coffee. Herr Schmidt wasn't stingy, on the contrary he believed that when it came to food items, quality had its price. The chubby gum-chewing clerk threw questions in his face that he cleverly dismissed with "Just the coffee." He didn't see why he should pay extra for milk when they had better milk at home. But he did buy a few rolls. He carried the paper bag down the street. Because he didn't want to spill anything, he was markedly slower on the way back. Mendel from the neighboring house stood at his kitchen window staring and smiling. Herr Schmidt ignored him. At home, he poured the bakery coffee into a clean cup, added milk, tasted it. It was cold.

Barbara was still lying in bed. She opened her eyes as he approached her side of the bed, where he otherwise never went. For a moment the perspective surprised him, he saw his own messy side of the bed, the indentation of the back of his head on the pillow. It still wasn't clear whether Barbara would manage to make the bed today. He handed her the coffee. She sat up on her elbows, tried it, and smiled a crooked smile.

"What?" asked Herr Schmidt. Only then did he notice a cut across her temple. He must have missed it before. It was already scabbed over, and he saw dried blood in her hair.

"Do you want to wash up?"

"Am I dirty?"

"Yes."

He found a pale blue washcloth in the bathroom and wetted it. Barbara wiped her mouth and the wrong side of her face.

"I'm a bit weak," she said.

"I can tell." He didn't want to sound cranky. He hadn't had any breakfast yet and had already walked as much as he normally did all day.

On the way to the kitchen again, Herr Schmidt walked past the phone that stood on a little side table in the hall, next to it a note with Karin's number and the list of numbers for the urgent care doctor, the family doctor, and the woman minister. Sebastian's number was in fourth position, despite the fact that he lived nearby, though unlike Karin he had a family.

Herr Schmidt didn't normally eat fleischwurst for breakfast, but he had no choice on this particular morning. He cut himself a thick slice. Of all the kitchen utensils, Herr Schmidt was handiest with the knife. He cut a pretzel roll, they were his favorite. The butter from the fridge proved hard, normally Barbara put it out as soon as she got up so it was waiting on the table at the right temperature. Herr Schmidt positioned a few yellow rectangles next to each other on the two halves of roll and then smeared some currant jam on top. Then he climbed the stairs yet again, nearly forgetting the plate. Barbara lay on her back, eyes closed, the damaged side of her face didn't look good. Herr Schmidt placed the plate on her stomach. She opened her eyes.

"I'm not myself today, Walter."

"You need to eat."

"Maybe later."

He reached with his hand and scratched the blood from her ear with the nail of his pointer finger. She didn't flinch. The fleischwurst hadn't sat well, it was too early for it, he needed his bread roll first. If Barbara wasn't going to eat hers, perhaps he could take a bite.

The butter was too thick, gave the jam a fatty aftertaste that filled his entire mouth, but the fresh pretzel roll made up for it. He ate the entire half, gallantly gulping down the butter clumps.

"Walter."

He flinched as if he'd been caught.

"I haven't cooked."

As if this wouldn't have occurred to him on his own. "It's still early."

"Have a look in the freezer. Take out the soup with meatballs."

He patted Barbara's blanket reassuringly, needed to say something nice to her, as miserable as she looked.

"That's my favorite."

"You have to warm it up first, you know."

Apparently she took him for an idiot.

"You have to eat, too, Barbara. I'll bring you another roll."

"Maybe later." She closed her eyes again.

The freezer chest was full, of course. Barbara had bought

it ten years before, when she said she no longer wanted to can everything, she wanted to freeze things, too. They had the garden, after all, and Karin had long since moved out by then. Sebastian didn't visit often either and all he ever took home with him was a jar of marmalade and even that he took with an expression as if he were doing Herr Schmidt a personal favor. Eleven jars from this year stood on the shelf and seven from the year before, Herr Schmidt didn't bother to keep count of the older ones.

Barbara had cooked too much of late, but perhaps they also ate less. Whatever was left over she froze so she could take a break now and then. Actually, though, she cooked every day regardless. One single time, four years ago, she took a trip to go hiking with one of her friends, without Herr Schmidt, and had left behind a list detailing which container he was supposed to defrost and when. Herr Schmidt hadn't been opposed to the trip, but still remembered the helpless rage that seized him when he opened to freezer and pulled out an ice-covered vessel that hurt his fingers, the contents of which he was supposed to defrost and warm up according to a precise set of instructions. In silent protest he hadn't followed Barbara's guidelines, and instead of goulash had eaten stuffed cabbage, assuming it would not go unnoticed, would perhaps even annoy her. But when she returned, radiant, in a great mood, and tan, she hadn't said a thing about it.

He opened the top of the freezer chest. The containers were carefully labeled with the dish and date. The soup with meatballs was on top, once again it hurt his fingertips to touch it. Herr Schmidt felt a brief flash of anger, though not as strong as the last time, more of a pinprick.

Barbara was never sick. In the first decade of their marriage he could barely believe it, because as a girl she hadn't looked very healthy, thin, blond hair, pale face. He had his doubts back then, because a sickly wife would have been just too much. But her outward appearance was deceptive, because inside she was made of steel. When she was pregnant with the children, she hadn't put her feet up a single time during the day, and two hours before giving birth she'd cleaned the kitchen. Each time she came home with a newborn baby, she immediately started cooking again. Once she had injured her wrist and had to cook left-handed, with thick bandages on the right. Even if she had made a bit of a mess of it as a result, Herr Schmidt never said a word.

Herr Schmidt filled the sink with hot water and submerged the container of frozen soup with meatballs. Helmut sat in front of his bowl and looked up at Herr Schmidt. Herr Schmidt looked back. Helmut whimpered and covered his muzzle with his paws.

Barbara held her hands in front of her eyes when Herr Schmidt opened the curtains. "The dog," he said, trying not to look directly at her face, because it still wasn't totally cleaned up.

"Oh," said Barbara, even sitting up a bit. Her paleness stood out even more as she suddenly flushed in spots. "His ground meat is in the plastic container in the refrigerator, you have to brown it."

"What do you mean, brown it?"

"Put it in the little pan, no oil, it's non-stick. Then add oats and a potato."

"But why brown it?"

"So he won't get sick."

"He's a dog. Dogs eat garbage."

"You know how his stomach is."

Herr Schmidt didn't know. "He doesn't eat canned food?"

"God forbid, Walter."

"You need to eat, too."

"Maybe later." She had closed her eyes again.

Helmut swatted him with his tail when Herr Schmidt entered the kitchen again.

"All right, all right."

Herr Schmidt opened the fridge. It was tidy, eggs and milk on the door, the butter dish still out. In a bowl covered with cling wrap were the potatoes, cooked skin-on, from the day before. On a plastic container was a note that read, "For Helmut." Did Barbara always have it like this, or had she already suspected yesterday that she was going to fall today? Herr Schmidt took off the lid, sniffed. Helmut romped around excitedly.

"Calm down!" shouted Herr Schmidt, to drown out the rumbling of his own stomach as much as anything else. He turned on the stove—child's play—put a pan on the burner, dumped in the contents of the plastic container. Nothing happened at first. Herr Schmidt sat down, picked up yesterday's newspaper. He'd forgotten today's in the newspaper box because of Barbara. He read the lead piece again, it was something about Britain. Something smelled burnt, the pan was steaming. Herr Schmidt got up and grabbed it from the stove. Even though part of the ground meat was burnt and the rest was raw, it smelled good. Helmut howled.

"Calm down!" Herr Schmidt put the pan back on the burner and began to stir it until all of the meat first lost its color and then browned. Before he shook it into the bowl, he put a bit on a plate and salted it.

"Careful, it's hot!" shouted Herr Schmidt as Helmut hurled himself at the meat. The dog didn't listen, let a few crumbs fall, and then licked them up immediately. The bowl was empty in seconds flat.

"Boy, are you stupid," said Herr Schmidt. "What are you going to do all day if you finish eating so quickly? Wait for dinner? You need to take it easy."

Helmut wagged his tail.

Herr Schmidt's gaze fell on the bowl of the potatoes. Barbara had mentioned them and said something about oats.

"You want potatoes?" He reached his hand out and showed Helmut a spud. "Look, from yesterday."

Helmut turned away.

"Have it your way." Herr Schmidt cut the potatoes as they were, cold and with the skin on, onto the meat on his plate, wondered if he should sprinkle oats on top, decided against it. He tried it and added more salt.

"You have it good with Barbara," he said when he was done. "She spoils you. And what's on the menu for tonight?"

Helmut didn't seem to know, either.

The day went by quickly. Herr Schmidt took Helmut out and then looked in again on Barbara, who still didn't want to eat anything. He considered calling Karin, but determined to wait on that until tomorrow. He checked to make sure everything was in order in the garden, but there was a lot to do, the blue and yellow crocuses looked feeble, the narcissuses had spread but weren't blooming yet. The pear tree stood there bare, its few buds shut tight. It was still too cold for the tomato and pepper seedlings. Barbara had planted them in yoghurt containers in the sunroom, yet again there were far too many.

Herr Schmidt solved a crossword puzzle and five sudokus, which were laughably easy, went out with Helmut, this time to the woods. It was still bearable on a workday, there was plenty of air and space. On weekends, by contrast, everyone went to the woods, and Barbara seemed to know every single one of them and needed to discuss something urgent with every second one.

Herr Schmidt hadn't taken even twenty steps before he was overtaken by a fat woman in a tracksuit, who swung ski poles around as she walked. When she was a good two meters ahead, she suddenly turned around, looked first at Helmut, then abruptly at Herr Schmidt.

"Walterrr!" she shouted with a heavy accent that caused Herr Schmidt bodily pain. The "r" rolled like rubble crashing down a mountain to engulf Herr Schmidt's peace of mind. "Where is Barrrbarrra, Walterrr?"

He didn't know this woman. Or perhaps he did? He felt as if he'd been caught out.

"She's relaxing," he eventually said.

"Is she underrr the weatherrr?"

Finally he realized this was Natalja, Barbara went belly-dancing with her, or whatever nonsense it was she did in her free time. Natalja sure had a belly. Suddenly it occurred to him that Barbara probably spoke Russian with Natalja when they met up, taking advantage of the fact that he wasn't there. He had been very strict with Barbara and her speech early on, and when he heard Natalja just now, he had to pat himself on the back retroactively. Unthinkable that Barbara might still talk like that today.

"How long have you lived in Germany?" he asked.

The fat woman looked skyward. "Let's count. Ten, twenty, twenty-one, twenty-four. Twenty-four years! Next year will be my silver anniversary with Germany." She beamed at him. "So what's the story with Barrrbarrra?"

"I don't know."

"Has she run off?" She found this funny. "Is she not going today?"

"Where?"

"The class."

"No, she won't be coming today."

"I'll call herrr."

"Best not."

"Did you kill her?" She looked serious for a split second before she laughed her horrible laugh again.

"No," said Herr Schmidt.

"That's good." She scratched Helmut on the top of his head, and Herr Schmidt got annoyed that the German Shepherd, which women were normally scared of, tolerated it. Barbara had coddled the dog too much. "Say hello to Barrrbarrra." Then off she went swinging her ski poles.

By evening, the meatball soup had not only thawed in the sink, it was room temperature. Herr Schmidt shared it with Helmut. When they were finished (Helmut much more quickly, though Herr Schmidt didn't dawdle, either), he thought of Barbara again. He hadn't been in the bedroom for hours. Barbara was asleep, the light was on in the bathroom. Apparently she'd gone to the bathroom at some point, Herr Schmidt realized hopefully. He turned off the light, sat down in front of the TV, and watched a western while Helmut lay at his feet and cringed at every gunshot. "It's just the TV," said Herr Schmidt, and Helmut twitched the tips of his gray-brown ears attentively. Herr Schmidt enjoyed watching the movie without Barbara's commentary, she considered movies with shoot-outs too brutal and only understood half of what went on anyway. He watched a second western, which came on right after the first, then went to bed.

Herr Schmidt had nightmares—about Sebastian. Once again he saw before his eyes the disappointed, slightly disgusted face of his son, and again didn't understand what the cause of it could be. Herr Schmidt sat up in bed. He had the impression he'd heard Sebastian's unhappy voice. He turned to the side, reached his hand out into emptiness. At first he was happy. It was typical for the other side of the bed to be empty when he woke up, and then the scent of coffee would waft up from below. But it was still dark out, and then he heard footsteps. Something slow and plodding was dragging itself from the bathroom into the bedroom. A hunched shadow formed in the doorframe and headed toward the bed. An old woman, like a witch out of a children's book, her nightgown glowing in the moonlight.

"Barbara?"

"Who else."

She sat down on the edge of the bed and pulled her legs up onto the mattress with a sigh.

"What's going on with you?" His voice was trembling all of a sudden.

"Nothing. I'm tired."

"Well, it is nighttime."

He didn't like her. This wasn't the Barbara he knew. He reached out his hand and touched her face. She jerked back, startled, but he was able to briefly feel her with his fingertips. Her skin was disagreeably cold and clammy.

"You're not going to die on me, are you, Barbara?"

She said nothing.

"You're still young!" he said, it was meant to sound stern but had a pleading undertone.

Now she laughed, which reminded him of the woman in the woods.

"Really," he insisted. "You're younger than I am."

"So?"

"I ran into that fat woman in the woods. Your friend. The Russian. She asked about you."

"And you?"

"What about me? Nothing. She thought I'd murdered you."

Barbara smiled, and Herr Schmidt felt a tension, that he hadn't even noticed, release.

"That fatty will die before you, the way she jiggles around."

"She's twenty years younger than I am."

"You're more attractive."

"Ridiculous." Barbara had laid her head back down onto the pillow, but now Herr Schmidt was wide awake.

"You going back to sleep? You slept all day." He tugged at the sleeve of her nightgown.

"I'm tired somehow."

He would like to have told her to knock it off with the tiredness. She had slept enough. But Barbara was stubborn even as a young woman, and with age it hadn't gotten any better.

"She speaks such poor German, your friend."

"It's just an accent. I have one, too."

"Yours isn't so bad. You don't even hear it. Imagine where we'd be if I hadn't have been so strict."

She remained silent.

"We'd be Russians, Barbara. And our children would be Russians. You could stick your German passport to your forehead—it wouldn't help."

"Get a hold of yourself." She turned onto her other side.

His mood, not particularly good before, had now irrevocably soured. Even at night Barbara could exasperate him so, even when she was so weak that he needed to worry she might not be as healthy as she had always looked, after he had nurtured her in the early years and kept at her about her speech so that other people would also treat her nicely. Without good German you were lost. She was a good student, at some stage she even suggested *he* was using certain words incorrectly because he didn't read as much as she did. She wanted to fight with him over proper German. She. With him. He felt his lips grudgingly curl into a smile.

"I need something sweet, Barbara."

"Look in the drawer," she mumbled without turning back to him.

"Which one?"

"My god, Walter. In the kitchen, right under the utensils."

Which meant he had to go down to the kitchen yet again. Not even at night could one have a bit of peace. He went barefoot, because he couldn't locate his slippers in the dark. On the stairs he put on the light, didn't want to fall and smash his skull, too. What a pair they'd make then, he and Barbara.

Helmut seemed happy to see him, and wagged his tail, but Herr Schmidt waved him away. "It's still nighttime, can't you tell?"

Helmut trotted back to his dog basket.

He had never opened this drawer. It was the secret drawer Barbara had created because he wasn't supposed to eat too many sweets on account of his stomach. Though he wasn't fat, just a normal man with a stout midsection. She gave him his ration when he wanted something sweet, and he put up with it. Now he felt like a little kid secretly taking a spoonful of grandma's marmalade. The drawer was full of packets of chocolate and cookies. He took the bar that was on top and carried it up to the bedroom, lay down in bed, crinkled it open.

"You want a piece, too, Barbara?"

She pretended to be asleep.

"You need to eat something." He placed the first square of chocolate on his tongue. It was milk chocolate, his favorite. Not dark chocolate, not chocolate with pepper or ginger or some other difficult to chew crap that Barbara liked. "Can you remember when you were new here and we'd just been married, had no money, and you sprinkled sugar on bread rolls and flicked a little water over the top and that was cake for us."

Barbara didn't answer. Herr Schmidt ate the entire bar, folded the paper into a small square, and put it on the nightstand. It had been too much chocolate, now he had an unsavory aftertaste in his mouth. Barbara would scold him in the morning if she noticed. He shoved the paper under his pillow so he could quickly dispose of it in the morning, before she made the bed.

* * *

Herr Schmidt slept in the next morning, which wasn't surprising; he had been up and about all night, after all. Helmut howled downstairs in the kitchen. Barbara didn't stir. He checked: she was breathing.

This time he didn't even bother trying to make coffee. He put Helmut's leash on and went straight to the bakery. He'd never been there so late in the day before. The display case was nearly empty, but he'd bought rolls yesterday. He ordered two coffees, black, and paid the unbelievable sum of 5.60 euros in coins.

"Too expensive," he said when the fat clerk handed him two plastic cups. "Why so expensive?"

"I don't set the prices," she said.

"Who buys something like this?"

"You, for one."

"Only because my wife can't make it herself at the moment."

The girl behind the counter looked at him from beneath giant lashes that reminded him of hairy caterpillars. "What's wrong with her?"

As if it was anything to her.

"If only I knew," said Herr Schmidt, ashamed by his own garrulousness. "Lying in bed, won't get up."

"Then she's probably depressed."

Herr Schmidt thought it over. "Don't know. She fell over in the bathroom yesterday."

"Maybe it's a circulatory issue. She should have a coffee."

"That's why I'm here." Despite himself Herr Schmidt told the tale of trying to make coffee the day before. The girl with the caterpillars on her face listened, occasionally shifting her chewing gum from one cheek to the other.

"It's not hard," she said. "You put in one spoonful per cup plus one for the pot. My grannie always used to put in a grain of salt, too."

"Why?"

"Everything tastes better with salt."

Herr Schmidt remembered the meat intended for Helmut

that he had salted. "Does this coffee have salt in it?" He gestured at the two cups.

"Nah. I just push a button and the machine does everything."

"For lazy people," scowled Herr Schmidt.

"Exactly."

The coffee in the cups was going to get cold, he couldn't waste the entire day.

He took Barbara the coffee, transferred into a proper cup, together with a jam-smeared roll, even though she hadn't asked for one. Barbara took the cup.

"It's cold," said Herr Schmidt.

"Doesn't matter. It tastes good." She took a sip and put down the cup.

"You have to eat something!"

"Later."

"Not later. Now." He took the roll with jam from the plate and tried to put it in her hand, but she wouldn't take it. Then he held it to her lips. "Open your mouth!"

"You're nuts, Walter."

"Open up. You know what happens to people who don't eat?"

She wanted to protest—she always had to battle with him—but at that moment he stuck the roll into her mouth. She bit off a piece and began to chew.

"I'm going to call Karin," said Herr Schmidt.

"Leave her be. She's busy."

"Maybe she can talk some sense into you."

"I'm just a little weak. I'll get up soon."

"That's what you said yesterday."

The next day was a Sunday. Herr Schmidt had no idea where Saturday had gone, all those slow hours he usually spent waiting for Barbara to come home from exercising, from meeting friends, or even just talking on the phone. Sometimes he tried to dissuade her, but since he'd retired, his words seemed to count for less. In the past he'd been able to get her to be brief on the phone by bringing up the bill, but these days talking on the phone didn't seem to cost a thing anymore, which was why everyone chattered to each other incessantly, took their devices shopping, to the gym, and even into the woods, where they jabbered on about this or that crap even while taking a walk. It was those moments when Herr Schmidt wished for a cane that he could use to knock the babble-devices out of their hands so they wouldn't continue to torture him. But he still didn't need a cane, he was still just fine on his own two feet.

Barbara's lying around in bed didn't agree with him. Things he had seemingly grown accustomed to now irritated him. On Sunday the baker was closed. But Herr Schmidt realized this only after he was standing in front of the storefront. Normally, closed shops provided him satisfaction: it had been normal in the past for shops not to be open around the clock, people just had to adapt. But when you hadn't yet had a coffee, it was less than ideal to be standing in front of a locked bakery door.

Herr Schmidt went back home, fed Helmut the veal goulash he'd thawed the day before, and then pensively took up a position in front of the coffee machine. The fat girl's granny must have known how to make coffee. He recited the recipe aloud, ladled two spoons of coffee into the filter and one more for the pot, salted it, poured in water, and pushed the button. It was child's play.

The coffee had an intense aftertaste, which wasn't banished by the milk, either. He took Barbara a cup. She sipped it cautiously. "It's hot today. And salty, if you ask me."

He had expected a bit more gratitude.

"The other coffee, the last few days, was from the bakery. 2.80 a cup."

"This is from the can in the kitchen, right?" she asked. "It's decaf and a bit stale. Usually I grind it fresh. The beans are in the bag in the refrigerator."

"You do what to it?"

"Grind it. With the coffee mill."

Herr Schmidt remembered the horrible daily rattle that always sent Helmut fleeing. Barbara handed him the empty cup. She didn't touch the bread roll.

He was unhappy that she took everything for granted. On the way to the kitchen he stopped at the telephone, picked up the handset, and dialed the number. He could have sworn that he dialed Karin, but Sebastian's annoyed voice said, "Schmidt."

"Father here," said Herr Schmidt, surprised.

Sebastian didn't say anything for quite some time. Herr Schmidt listened as something at the other end of the line was loudly moved, as if Sebastian were rearranging the furniture while talking on the phone. Herr Schmidt gave in first.

"Where are you?"

"At the office."

"It's Sunday."

"I know."

"I can call you on your normal phone."

"This is my normal phone."

"It must cost a fortune."

"Quit it."

Herr Schmidt could practically see Sebastian gritting his teeth and forcing out the sentences.

"Everything okay with you guys?" Sebastian finally asked.

Herr Schmidt took a breath. "It's still cool outside," he began, but Sebastian interrupted him.

"I can see for myself what the weather is like. Has something happened? Where is Mama?"

"I killed her," said Herr Schmidt.

"What?"

"Joking. She's tired, lying in bed."

"Mama's in bed?"

Sebastian's agitation provided Herr Schmidt with hard-won satisfaction. It confirmed that he had been through something unimaginable in the last few days.

"Is she breathing?"

"Of course she's breathing," said Herr Schmidt, annoyed. "She even talks."

"Thank god. Put her on the phone."

"Can't, she's in the bedroom."

"I gave you that cordless phone."

"I'm in the hallway, on the normal phone."

"Father, you drive me crazy."

Although he would have preferred to have heard a friendly word from Sebastian, he was secretly pleased by this. Any emotional exertion was better than indifference.

"You hang up, and I'll call you back on Mama's mobile. Then you can take it to her."

"She's asleep."

"God damn it!" shouted Sebastian, and Herr Schmidt jumped, startled, causing him to drop the phone. This was an indisputable advantage of normal telephones: it didn't fall to the floor, instead it hung from the cord and swung gently back and forth. Sebastian's voice was no longer audible. Herr Schmidt waited a few moments, then hung up.

The phone rang immediately. Herr Schmidt answered: "I'm still on the same phone."

"What?" It wasn't Sebastian, but Karin. "What's the story over there? What's going on with Mama?"

"How do you know about it?"

"How do you think?"

"Why would he call you rather than just coming over? He has a car, for god's sake."

"You already know."

"No, I don't," said Herr Schmidt, who was gradually finding all of this a bit too much. "I didn't kill your mother."

Karin exhaled loudly. "I already heard. That's good news."

"Yeah. Bye."

"Papa! Wait a minute."

Karin's voice was like honey—they had good honey from a beekeeper in the pantry, he was hungry again—and he felt like a fly stuck in it. He gave up any resistance and told her everything that had happened in the last three days, these three days without breakfast and a proper lunch.

"I just made coffee," Herr Schmidt ended his report.

"What?"

"With the coffee machine."

"Okay," said Karin after a pause. "And how was it?"

"How should it have been? Salty."

"Okay," said Karin. "Is Mama able to talk?"

"Yes. She thought it was salty, too."

"Okay. Hasn't she gotten up at all?"

"She went to the bathroom overnight. Didn't fall over this time."

"Fall over?! Did she hurt herself?"

"She had blood on her head, but she's cleaned up. She washed it off. Don't get excited."

Karin was silent.

"Karin? Are you still there?"

"Yes. I'm googling the train connections. Shit, why does this have to happen now, of all times. I'm going to call Sebastian again."

"Don't call him," said Herr Schmidt, who now felt a bit ashamed that he had already called Sebastian and been screamed at by him.

"Something's wrong. I don't understand what is going on. Call a doctor immediately."

"It's Sunday."

"Call the emergency doctor."

"It's not an emergency. She drank my coffee."

Karin groaned. Herr Schmidt suddenly remembered that as a little girl she sometimes stole candies from the kitchen.

"Calm down," he told her, as if she were Helmut. "You don't need to come over."

"But there's something wrong about it all."

"We have food in the freezer."

"That I believe."

"We could surely live off it for a year. Stay in Berlin."

He heard her simultaneously laughing and sniffling.

"Papa, you have to promise me that tomorrow you'll call a doctor."

"I'll call Maschke. I'll go over and fetch him."

"Calling will suffice. He'll come over. Promise me."

"Yes, yes," he mumbled.

Herr Schmidt heard the relief in Karin's voice. "And are you still friends with Mai?" he asked before hanging up. He had struggled to come to terms with the name for years, all to no avail.

Karin paused. "Yes," she said. "Make sure Mama gets enough liquids, okay?"

When they finally hung up, Herr Schmidt was bathed in sweat and had to lie down. He went into the bedroom and stretched out next to Barbara—she had it easy, her third day in bed already. She lay on her back, Herr Schmidt turned to her, saw her sharp profile, her nose pointing at the ceiling. He got a cold chill.

"Barbara!" He shook her shoulder. "Are you there?"

She turned her head in his direction. "What?"

He sat up, leaned over her. Her face had changed, her skin was pale, nearly translucent, dark shadows beneath her eyes, as if she hadn't slept enough.

"You have to eat!"

"Maybe later."

"No! Not later." He shook her shoulder again, perhaps too hard: her head wobbled back and forth. He took his hand away again. "You're not going to starve on me. The freezer's full, what do you want to have? Everything's in there."

"I know. It'll be enough for a long time."

"Goulash? *Maultaschen*?"

"Wait a minute."

He waited. Her face was concentrating, as if she were listening to her insides. Herr Schmidt remembered that she actually cooked fresh daily only because she herself didn't like all the defrosted stuff. But she just couldn't throw out all the leftovers. What did she like? She had told him a few times in recent years. He wracked his brain. The name of the foreign stuff evaded him, but he kept thinking. "I can go get you one of those curries. Or sushi."

"Wait." She sat up, propped herself on her elbows. "Can you make me a potato?"

"A potato?"

"Yes. Simple, with butter and salt."

"How do you do that?"

"Ach, Walter. In water, in a pot."

He didn't like the way she explained things to him. When she clarified something for Henry, their grandchild, she smiled while doing so. Now she seemed annoyed, but she needn't be so condescending, because the fact was she wanted something from him.

"Where are the potatoes, anyway?"

"In the pantry. In a basket. You don't have to peel it."

He felt his entire body bristling. Barbara's explanation belittled him.

Even the advice of the fat girl at the bakery was easier to accept.

"How hot should the water be? What temperature?"

"Ach, Walter."

"How long should it stay in?"

"Until it's done."

He began to boil inside himself. "How will I know it's done?"

"Stick a fork in it."

He had never noticed how imprecisely she formulated things. If she had looked as robust as usual, he would have been upset. But the bout of panic as she'd lain in the bathroom had left its mark, like a wave that had crashed over him and then receded. Deep inside he was still wet and freezing.

"I'll make you a goddamn potato."

He boiled all nine of them to make it worthwhile. Scrubbed them beforehand with the brush, because dirt still clung to them. Where did Barbara get such filthy potatoes, their own were long gone, they'd eaten them all winter. Barbara had insisted on using the last of the homegrown potatoes, no matter how wizened and soft they'd gotten, and she'd tossed all the pinkish-white sprouted peels in the compost. He'd probably be able to dig magnificent tubers out of there come late summer.

The potatoes took forever. Herr Schmidt set the timer, sat down at the kitchen table, and watched the stove. Just bringing the water to a boil took a few minutes. He took a piece of paper and wrote *coffee* on it in large letters, jotted down the amount per cup, the salt, and then in parenthesis: *doesn't take long*. The ground meat that he'd sautéed for Helmut had also been more than palatable, and for that, too, he jotted down the ingredients. The defrosted foods didn't count. How long potatoes took would soon be apparent. He watched the pot. Now and then he stuck a fork into a potato. At the end the spuds were full of holes, the peels hung down. Herr Schmidt placed a potato on the prepositioned plate, cut a large pat of butter. At this rate the butter wasn't going to last long.

Barbara positioned a pillow behind her and took the plate

on her lap. Steam rose from the potato, the butter had melted into a golden puddle.

"Salt?" she asked.

The salt was still in the kitchen.

"It's fine, stay here."

And he did, after all he wasn't a servant. But as she dunked a piece of potato in the butter, he couldn't hold out any longer, down the stairs, back up the stairs.

"Why the whole package? Where's our salt shaker?"

"Are you never satisfied?"

It seemed to taste good to her. She savored each bite, he watched her, spellbound.

"Like the old days," she said. "When I was little. Do you remember?"

Herr Schmidt wanted to say that they hadn't known each other when she was little, but nodded instead.

"You want some, too?"

He nodded again, took the fork from her hand and put it in his mouth, squashing the hot, buttery morsel of potato with his tongue.

He wanted to give the fork back to Barbara, but she waved it away.

"Already finished? Doesn't it taste good?"

"Yes, it does. But I'm already full."

Again he felt the trembling, the lurking panic.

"You haven't eaten for days, look at yourself!"

"I have enough fat on me, I can last a few days."

"No you can't. You're getting thinner and thinner."

"Walter, why are you shouting?"

"I'm not shouting!" he yelled. "You have to eat. We're all starving."

He paused. Barbara squinted and reached out for the fork.

"That's it," said Herr Schmidt as she shoved small bites of the potato into her mouth. "Soak up the butter. You can get that last bite down."

"I can't eat anymore. It's normal, Walter, to eat less when you're sick."

"So you're sick? And won't say?"

Herr Schmidt suddenly saw an old woman in his mind's eye, she had snow-white hair, pressed her lips together, and held a spoon to his mouth. *Food makes you strong. You must always eat, Walter.* He was sick, lying feverish in bed, perhaps he had measles or scarlet fever. The old woman seemed to know, however, that he would survive just as long as he munched.

Herr Schmidt sat down in front of the television, in bright daylight, as if he were unemployed. He had forgotten to take off his outdoor shoes, and he put up his feet, just as they were, on a leather stool he'd slid close to the couch. Nothing but crap on TV, some random people were fighting, a face appeared on a talk show that Herr Schmidt found off-putting in an oddly familiar way, so he immediately changed the channel. Now he had to watch as a not-so-young couple pressed up against each other. The least objectionable program showed a plump man in an apron, peeling potatoes. Herr Schmidt got caught up and followed the deft movements of his short fingers on the screen. The man was talking about something that had nothing to do with his current task, it was about New York in the seventies. Herr Schmidt turned off the sound and watched as a snakelike strip came loose from the potato and fell into the sink, next spud, next strip. The peel transformed into a perfect, razor-thin, nearly translucent spiral, it was thrilling.

"Barbara, look!" shouted Herr Schmidt, as if she could hear him.

* * *

The next morning he was tired. Barbara was sleeping. Herr Schmidt realized that he would now have to look for the beans and coffee grinder, and that he had actually liked the taste of the stale decaf coffee, which probably had to do with the salt.

"Barbara," he whispered softly.

She didn't say anything, but she was breathing.

He must have fallen back to sleep; when he opened his eyes again, the doorbell was ringing like mad. A package, no doubt. Sometimes, no matter how much he scolded her for it, Barbara ordered ridiculous things online. Good that she couldn't go to the door now, that way he could just refuse delivery.

Herr Schmidt went, as he was, in striped pajamas, down the stairs, step by step, threw open the door, and discovered Dr. Maschke.

"What do you want?" asked Herr Schmidt. "I didn't even call you."

Maschke's practice was two blocks away, and he was a snooty bastard. He combed his sparse hair across his bald spot, and Herr Schmidt suspected he dyed it, too, as that sheen wasn't natural. Maschke couldn't have been much younger than Herr Schmidt himself, because he had already been practicing when Sebastian was little. When Herr Schmidt passed by Maschke's house with Helmut in the morning, the guy was always in his yard doing calisthenics, which he interrupted every time to ask Herr Schmidt when he was going to remember to drop in for a checkup. Herr Schmidt, however, never thought for a moment of having himself poked and prodded by Maschke.

"Your daughter called," said Maschke. "May I?"

Herr Schmidt stepped aside. Maschke entered, put down his ridiculous bag, took off his checkered jacket. "So where's your wife?"

"Sleeping," said Herr Schmidt.

"Then let's have a look." Without any further cues, Maschke headed up the stairs. Herr Schmidt watched him climb until his back hurt. Then he poured himself a glass of water from the kitchen sink and carried it up behind Maschke. In the bedroom, Barbara was smiling up at Maschke from a half-lying position as he took her hand and then ran his finger down to her wrist, his eyes riveted on his watch.

"Water," said Herr Schmidt loudly, handing Barbara the glass. Maschke looked up with a scowl. Barbara handed the glass on to him.

"Now I've lost count." Maschke gave the glass of water back to Herr Schmidt. Herr Schmidt sat down on the other side of the bed and cleared his throat. "So what does she have?"

Maschke pulled out a blood pressure sleeve and a stethoscope. Herr Schmidt had to wait. After taking her blood pressure, Maschke leaned in closer to Barbara, felt her neck, and began to speak to her quietly. Barbara alternately nodded and shook her head. They seemed determined that Herr Schmidt not understand them. He knew this game from his children.

"What does she have, Maschke?" he asked loudly.

Maschke looked at him, and Herr Schmidt got goose bumps.

"Bring your wife to the office."

Barbara looked over at Herr Schmidt and gently shook her head. Herr Schmidt glared at Maschke like a potato bug that was threatening his crops. "And why should I do that?"

"I can examine her properly there."

"Why's it better than here?"

"I have only limited equipment here."

"And what if she doesn't want to?"

"Would it be possible for me to have a glass of water, as well?" Maschke had stood up and was smiling awkwardly at Barbara as he took his leave.

Downstairs, Maschke looked around as if he'd never seen a kitchen before. "Do you have anyone to assist you?"

"What do you mean?"

"Do you have help around the house?"

"Why would we? Barbara does everything herself. The

freezer's fully stocked." Herr Schmidt filled a glass at the faucet, he had to act like a waiter for Maschke now, too. Maschke took the glass, said thank you, and put it down on the table without even taking a sip.

"Bring her to the office," he said again, slowly and seriously. "Convince her. Tell her that you'll call an ambulance otherwise."

"But it's not an emergency."

"And we don't want it to become one."

"She doesn't want to eat," said Herr Schmidt, noticing with disgust that his voice quivered slightly, like a little girl's. "I tried to get a potato down her. Homemade."

Maschke seemed unimpressed. "Fluids are important. Electrolytes. You understand what I mean?"

Herr Schmidt felt attacked. "I just took her water. Can *you* cook?"

"A little," said Maschke absentmindedly. "Please bring your wife's health insurance card, too, she hasn't been in this quarter. And I want to personally remind you to come in for a checkup. You really need one."

Barbara was always going for checkups, thought Herr Schmidt as he closed the door behind Maschke. And now she didn't want to eat.

That night he woke up and saw that Barbara was sitting up in bed. No wonder she couldn't sleep at night when she laid around all day. He touched her nightgown: "What is it?"

"*Grießbrei*," she said softly.

"What?"

"Cream of wheat. When I was sick as a child, there was always cream of wheat."

Herr Schmidt tried to remember how he used to eat it. "With sugar and cinnamon?"

"No!" How could a voice sound so weak and at the same time so indignant? "With currant jam."

"Nothing in your childhood home was the same as normal people's."

Barbara suddenly lay back down and pulled the covers up to her chin. But now Herr Schmidt was restless. Finally he got up and went down to the kitchen, searching the cabinets while Helmut looked on grumpily, finding a half-empty package of cream of wheat. He read the directions carefully, once out loud and once to himself, turned on the light above the stove, measured out cream of wheat and milk, put the two things in a pot and started to stir. Nothing happened. Annoyed, he sat down and picked up yesterday's newspaper with the crossword puzzle still not solved. By the fourth word, there was hissing and a foul smell, the milk had boiled over onto the stove and burnt, in the pot was a sticky mass of irregular clumps. Herr Schmidt put the hissing pot in the sink and went back to bed.

* * *

"You have to stir it," said the chubby girl with chewing gum in her mouth.

"I did."

"You have to stir it for a while. Until it thickens."

"How long?"

"No idea. A few minutes anyway."

"That's what I did."

"Then you have to do it for longer. Takes practice. But if you don't stir it right, you might as well not do it at all. Nobody wants lumpy Grießbrei."

"I don't want lumpy Grießbrei, either. I hated that as a kid."

She shrugged. The people behind him were getting impatient.

"How do you know everything?" asked Herr Schmidt suspiciously. "First the coffee, and now the stirring."

She rolled her eyes and blew a pink bubble.

He left the bakery without having bought anything. Making

coffee was going alright at this point, and they had enough bread rolls, though Herr Schmidt had forgotten to freeze them. They'd gotten hard, but he could depend on his teeth, even much younger folks could envy him that.

The dirty pot sat alongside the other dishes in the sink, but they had plenty of other pots. He repeated his measuring procedure from the previous day and began to stir. He hadn't expected to have to stir for so long. His arm hung heavy, and if he'd been younger he would have been bored. The cream of wheat swirled in the milk, maybe it had gone off because they'd had it around so long. But then, just as Herr Schmidt was contemplating giving up, something happened. The milk disappeared, and instead a viscous mass began to slow the whisk's progress. Herr Schmidt yanked the pot from the burner.

"Barbara! Look!"

He spooned some into a polka-dotted cereal bowl and nearly ran upstairs, stumbled on the middle step, and just barely managed to right himself by grabbing the bannister with his free hand. Because he'd forgotten a spoon and the currant jam, he had to go straight back down. He had awakened Barbara with his shouting, and now he held the bowl out to her. "Grießbrei!"

Like an ill-mannered child she stuck her finger into the cream of wheat and then licked it. Then she put out her hand for the spoon.

"I stirred and stirred," said Herr Schmidt, out of breath.

"It's a little thick."

Of course, she was never satisfied. Even so, she ate it all. Herr Schmidt felt as though cream of wheat were swirling inside his chest.

"We had to economize," she said more to herself than to Herr Schmidt. "Watered down the milk."

"I didn't water it down."

"You made this yourself?"

Herr Schmidt sat down. "Who did you think made it? Helmut?"

"You made Grießbrei for me?"

They looked at each other. Barbara blinked. One side of her chestnut-dyed hair was matted down and the other puffed up comically.

"As if it were an art form," said Herr Schmidt hoarsely.

"It took me a long time," said Barbara after a pause. "Before I could cook halfway decently."

"You don't have to tell me."

He smiled at the memory. At first she'd been completely incompetent. She was a young woman and had looked even younger. It had required a lot of patience as she tried to learn to cook. She managed to make scrambled eggs taste like the bottom of a shoe—and eggs weren't free, either. She tried to make soups, which he bravely ate. She herself didn't even manage it, he saw her gag. She used handwritten recipes from her mother and grandmother and cursed: nothing worked. The flour was different, the quark runnier than she was used to, you couldn't work with it. Not that she would have complained, but he could see on her face the guilty feelings mixed with despair. He'd had no sympathy: all other women somehow managed to keep their husbands fed. Only Barbara let pancakes burn in the pan, and only her lentil dishes put your teeth at risk.

His mother had been upset, said he'd starve, said other unpleasant things about Barbara. It pained him that she considered the marriage a betrayal of everything the family had fought for. He'd forbidden himself to think about it, he'd simply had no choice. At some stage they would get used to it, that's how things in life had always been and this was no different.

He'd decided back then to give Barbara time, one year. After six months things at least improved in the kitchen. The noodles no longer stuck together. She learned to put a bit of butter in, a habit she later abandoned when she decided they'd all gotten too fat.

When he thought back on it now, it felt unreal, like a movie he'd seen many years ago. He took the empty bowl from her, went down to the kitchen, sat down, and scraped the pot. There was some charring this time, too, but the burnt bits tasted particularly good, not like cream of wheat, more like a baked good with caramel. When he'd finished the pot gleamed, scraped clean with the spoon. How long had he had to stir it in the end? Herr Schmidt scrounged up a pen and scribbled a note: Grießbrei. Barbara had been right: a little thinner would have been better. He measured out slightly more milk and put the pot back on the burner.

* * *

He took the dog out. Mendel's aging mother hunched in the front yard weeding, though there were no weeds to be seen. She stood upright to say hello to Herr Schmidt. Unlike Mendel the son, she was polite.

Herr Schmidt walked Helmut on a short leash because people were afraid of German Shepherds. Which was good. Though Helmut was actually as gentle as a lamb, Barbara had spoiled him, turned him into a lapdog that everyone was allowed to pet when he was still a puppy. No wonder, then, that later on he didn't make much of a watchdog. When they got the next dog, Herr Schmidt would take things into his own hands again.

He took a series of lefts until he was beyond the housing development. Crossing a somewhat larger street, he arrived at the market square, with a row of shops, a pizzeria, and an ice cream parlor. When you crossed the square, followed the main road, and turned left, you ended up at a small patch of woods with a public ping-pong table in the middle where the useless teens hung around, talked like idiots, and took drugs. Not far beyond was the S-bahn station, in front of which stood a lone high-rise that Herr Schmidt detested more than all the other buildings he knew. In principle, he didn't have anything against the Turks who made up the majority of the building's residents, at least not against all of them. Some of them were hard-working people, which he respected. Most of them, however, couldn't even parent their own children—where could they find the time when they were always working illegally. In front of the high-rise stood a grubby concrete box that referred to itself as a youth cultural center. If upstanding girls came home in the evening on the S-bahn after a day out in the city, they had their parents or big brothers pick them up, specifically because of the youth cultural center. No woman wanted to run into the shady types who hung out there after sunset.

Only when he was standing in front of the Golden Stag did Herr Schmidt manage to rouse himself from his thoughts. It was Thursday, and the annex with the bowling alley was already lit up. Herr Schmidt could see through the window that the men were already there. Günther, John, Klaus. One spot was still free, it was his. He pictured going in, how they'd greet him loudly, more loudly than necessary, because none of them could hear very well anymore. They'd pet Helmut, Helmut would piss himself out of joy, and Herr Schmidt would feel ashamed of the entire breed. Then the dog would crawl under the bench. Hanne, the hostess, would bring Herr Schmidt a beer and Helmut a piece of sausage. The men would grin at Hanne with their dentures. They wouldn't ask Herr Schmidt about Barbara because that wasn't appropriate here. After all, they didn't ask Klaus how it was going without his wife, either. They just pressed on, which was the appropriate way to go about things.

Herr Schmidt held the leash taut, felt Helmut's excitement. He heard Hanne laughing inside. But Herr Schmidt walked away, pulling the dog behind without looking at him. The last thing he needed right now was to see his look of disappointment.

Back home he sat down in front of the television and watched the little fat guy as he stirred some green stuff in a pan. All around his workspace stood little bowls filled with ingredients Herr Schmidt couldn't identify. The chef talked too much and most of what he said had nothing to do with the task at hand. His high, feminine voice annoyed Herr Schmidt, he muted the sound. But then he was overwhelmed by the feeling that he might be missing some vital piece of information. As soon as he had turned the sound back on, he was subjected to some nonsense about picking your own herbs. The show's superfluous background music became suffused with a whimpering undertone. Then Herr Schmidt realized the noise was coming from Helmut. When Helmut made a noise like he was being slaughtered, it usually meant he was happy. When Karin visited, for instance, Helmut reacted as soon as the car turned onto their street.

"Quiet!" Herr Schmidt yelled, but Helmut still couldn't control himself. Karin's in Berlin, mumbled Herr Schmidt, peeling himself out of the leather couch. He walked into the foyer and abruptly halted. Helmut was prancing around Sebastian, who had just taken off his jacket and was now petting the dog.

"Quiet," said Herr Schmidt. "You hysterical hound."

Sebastian hung his jacket in the coat closet. "Decided not to ring the bell. Thought you might still be sleeping."

"I'm not sleeping." Herr Schmidt hadn't been prepared for Sebastian. It felt too cramped in the foyer with his son, actually it felt too cramped anywhere with his son.

"I'll turn off the television," said Herr Schmidt.

"Okay," said Sebastian.

Herr Schmidt slumped back into the leather couch in the living room and reached for the remote. The fat guy on the screen was now whipping cream, which was good because he couldn't talk while doing it. The mixer made a racket, Herr Schmidt muted the sound again. The camera showed a bowl where a white fluid was transforming into something new, something foamy and porous, which always struck Herr Schmidt as bordering on magic, that is, if he actually believed in such nonsense.

"What are you watching?" Sebastian sat down on the couch, too, at the other end.

"Nothing, really," said Herr Schmidt vaguely.

"What happened to the kitchen?"

"Nothing."

"Terrific conversation," said Sebastian. "Is Mama sleeping?"

"No. She ate some Grießbrei. I made it." Before Sebastian could get off another stupid comment, Herr Schmidt preempted him: "Would you like some?"

"The kitchen's completely out of hand, Father. Everything's a mess, spilled milk, the fridge door's even standing open. You need somebody."

"What do you mean?"

"Somebody to help around the house."

"Your mother won't put up with another woman in the house."

Sebastian leaned back and took a deep breath.

"So do you want Grießbrei or not?" asked Herr Schmidt irritably. On the TV screen the fat guy was now adding melted chocolate to the whipped cream, it was an intoxicating sight. "What's he doing? Barbara's never made anything like that."

"Of course she has. That's chocolate pudding. We had it every Saturday with raspberries."

"That's not pudding. Look at it. That's just whipped cream with chocolate. Just two things mixed together."

"O.K., then it's chocolate mousse."

"How do you know that?"

Again a deep breath and an unnecessarily long pause. "What'd you say about Grießbrei a minute ago, Father?"

They went to the kitchen together. Helmut jumped around Sebastian and nipped playfully at his hand. Herr Schmidt suddenly saw the kitchen from Sebastian's perspective and understood what he must have meant. Sebastian put on Barbara's apron—he had on a snow-white shirt and crisply ironed pants, after all—and started to load the dishwasher. Herr Schmidt felt superfluous, just as when Barbara was in the kitchen. He sat down and watched Sebastian load the machine.

"So where's this Grießbrei, Father? And what is this?"

What was left of the cream of wheat had hardened in the pot. Sebastian was picky, he probably wouldn't eat it. Herr Schmidt waved his hand. Sebastian hung up the now damp towel, the motion was all Barbara. People always said that Sebastian looked like Herr Schmidt, they practically insisted, as if he had any reason to doubt it. But whenever he looked at his son, he saw Barbara. Sure, he may have had Herr Schmidt's hair color, but his gestures and his overly sensitive temperament could only have come from his mother.

Herr Schmidt squinted. He had no sense of how much time it took to make the kitchen sparkling clean.

"Does your . . . also not clean up around the house?" asked Herr Schmidt. He didn't know what to call her. Sebastian always got upset, regardless of what word Herr Schmidt used for her.

"Who?"

"You know."

"She has a name."

"I can't pronounce it."

"Listen closely." Sebastian said it slowly. It must have been at least thirteen syllables.

"I already said I can't pronounce it."

Sebastian shrugged. "Have you already had breakfast?" He inspected the refrigerator, pulled out a carton of eggs, and turned them over so he could read the expiration date. Herr

Schmidt watched with a furrowed brow as Sebastian put a frying pan on the stove, as four eggs ran toward each other, as the clear egg whites quickly turned opaque and white. It seemed ridiculously easy. Herr Schmidt reached for a pen and piece of paper.

"What are you doing?"

"Nothing. Taking notes."

The table was already set. They sat across from one another and ate in silence. Sebastian had cut the hard bread rolls into slices and browned them in the pan. They were greasy and sticky and had to be eaten with knife and fork.

"I'm taking Mama to the doctor," said Sebastian when they had finished.

"Maschke was here."

"I know. She needs to see a specialist."

Herr Schmidt basically shared this opinion, but he felt the need to contradict on principle. "Barbara has been going to Maschke since you were little."

"That was his father. Maschke Junior isn't that old."

"I thought he was the same age as me."

Sebastian said nothing.

"I can't convince your mother."

"Since when?"

"What?"

"Since when can't you convince her?" Sebastian mopped up a last bit of egg yolk from the plate and stuffed the last bite of bread roll in his mouth. "I'll go with her to the doctor."

"That's not necessary. I can take her."

"Is it okay if I sleep here?"

Herr Schmidt chewed on his lower lip. "And what will . . . your . . . say to that?"

"She has a name."

"I can't pronounce it. Do whatever you want."

* * *

For the next few days he felt like a guest in his own house. Sebastian was everywhere at once, and didn't feel any need to ask Herr Schmidt for permission. Once when he'd been in the kitchen for a long time, Herr Schmidt stuck his head in the door: "What're you doing in there?"

"Nothing."

"I heard something."

"Normally you never hear anything."

Then Sebastian sat for hours with Barbara in the bedroom, whispering with her, depriving her of any peace and quiet. When Herr Schmidt trudged up the stairs, he found Barbara asleep and Sebastian on a chair next to her, fiddling with his phone.

"You'll disturb her. She'll never get back on her feet."

"Then don't talk so loud, you'll wake her up."

"She needs to eat something."

Sebastian looked back down at his phone. "Shall we order something?"

"How?"

"From a restaurant. Delivery."

"We don't have that sort of thing around here."

"Of course you do." Sebastian stood up and held the phone out to Herr Schmidt, showing him photos of various sorts of noodles.

"I don't eat that kind of stuff."

Once again a deep breath. Sebastian sat back down, straightened Barbara's covers, continued to fiddle with his phone.

"I simply don't believe it," said Sebastian when Herr Schmidt opened the freezer chest. "You preparing for World War III?"

"What?"

"Nothing."

They had pulled out nine containers and lined them up on the counter. Red cabbage from Christmas two years before, goulash, beef stew.

"You can take something home," said Herr Schmidt. "For your . . . and the kid."

"Thanks, but we're fine."

"He has to eat, too."

Sebastian lowered his head and tried to read the already faded writing on a sticker.

"Pancakes with quark filling," said Herr Schmidt.

"I don't remember those at all," said Sebastian. "Can you even freeze something like that?"

Herr Schmidt shrugged. "It's her stuff, from back then," he said. "Old recipes from abroad." He had to resist spitting on the floor. After all, this was his home and his floor.

Sebastian opened the Tupperware container and sniffed the rolled-up pancakes covered with ice crystals. "Yeah, you hated that. Always got so dramatic about it. Why was that, anyway?"

"I didn't get dramatic. It's just not necessary to cook that sort of thing when you're here. There's enough normal German food."

"Here we go again," said Sebastian.

"What?"

"Nothing."

"Why am I not allowed to say that I don't want to eat beets?"

"I'll take the borscht," said Sebastian. "If it's still good."

"What could possibly happen to it."

It was always like this with Sebastian: either they said nothing or they fought. Herr Schmidt was in a bad mood now. Sebastian was always in a bad mood, and as sensitive as a mimosa plant; there wasn't a single word that didn't elicit that strange look from him. As if Herr Schmidt had done something to him.

"You can see we're doing fine. You needn't waste your time here with us."

"I brought work with me. As I mentioned, I need to take Mama to the doctor."

"I can do that myself."

"Yes, you can. But *I'm* going to do it. For dinner I'll be having pancakes with quark filling."

"You're nearly forty years old and you still act like a child."

"You're one to talk."

For the rest of the day they didn't speak to each other. Herr Schmidt waited for the show with the fat chef, Sebastian made himself toast with honey even though Herr Schmidt told him that Barbara had frozen at least five different kinds of cake. Once Barbara opened her eyes and asked for tea. Herr Schmidt, who didn't drink tea, let Sebastian make it, though he did take her a warm potato afterwards and ask where the TV guide was, because the one by the television was from last week.

"I haven't bought the new one yet," said Barbara, and Sebastian looked as if Herr Schmidt had once again said something wrong.

"Would you happen to know when the show with the fat chef comes on?"

Sitting halfway up, Barbara rolled the potato around her plate with her fork like a spoiled child being forced to eat. "What's his name?"

"How should I know," said Herr Schmidt. "He didn't introduce himself to me."

"Medinski. He watches Medinski now," said Sebastian.

"I've watched it twice," Herr Schmidt corrected, always striving to be truthful. "Three times at most. Is that his name? Is he a Pole?"

Barbara closed her eyes, Sebastian took a deep breath.

The show with the fat Pole apparently came on irregularly, all the reruns made it difficult to figure out. Sebastian and Herr

Schmidt went to the den, where Barbara had done the accounting in the past, and where she still kept financial records and old invoices in binders, and turned on the computer. It belonged to Barbara; Karin and Sebastian had given it to her, she'd taken two classes at the community college and learned how to use it. Even so, Herr Schmidt strictly forbid her to send money over the Internet, there were always warnings on TV about doing that.

Sebastian clicked around a bit and then opened a page for Herr Schmidt where the fat guy from the TV show grinned out at him.

"That's him," said Herr Schmidt.

"Wait. Do you see this button here? The guy's on Facebook. And Mama is, too, I had no idea. Look, we're automatically logged in."

They sat next to each other in front of the screen, Herr Schmidt in Barbara's chair, Sebastian on a yoga ball that also belonged to Barbara. Herr Schmidt saw a chaotic jumble of words and boxes, and in between were photos, most of which showed their garden, the flourishing plant beds, but in a few Herr Schmidt himself could also be seen: with his bicycle, with a glass of beer in his hand. Above the whole thing stood Barbara's name.

"What am I doing here on the computer?"

"Mama posted it. My god, we're being nosy. We could read all her messages. You think she might be cheating on you? Joking. Look, two people liked your photo."

"What does that mean? And who?"

"Carola Buch and Dietmar Günther."

"Günther saw it?"

"We could set up a page for you." Sebastian seemed to be having fun with all of this.

"What would I do with it?"

Sebastian did something to the screen, and suddenly Medinski was back, in his chef's apron.

"So, again, this is his Facebook page," said Sebastian. "You can click on all the videos, anything you might have missed on TV. And other stuff, too, bonus material. And underneath are the comments, you can say what you particularly like about it there."

"Why would I do something so ridiculous?"

"Fine, write what you found particularly stupid then."

"Good."

Sebastian clicked on the first video. Medinski had arranged all sorts of ingredients on the counter: eggs, milk, light brown nobs he referred to as mushrooms, a couple of tomatoes. He was saying you could recognize a good chef by the lightness of his omelets, then he broke the eggs into a bowl and beat them with a whisk, for quite a long time, the fluid turning to foam. Herr Schmidt ran his hand around the table, finding a pen and piece of paper. By the time he looked up, Sebastian was gone.

Herr Schmidt took his bicycle to go shopping, he had purposefully not told anyone. Barbara needed something fresh. He was beginning to believe less in the daily portion of frozen food than he let on to himself or to Sebastian. He hadn't said goodbye because he suspected Sebastian might have wanted to come if he had. Herr Schmidt hated going shopping, even with Barbara, and with Sebastian it would surely have been worse still: he would comment on everything and rush him, never leave him in peace to find the right stuff and compare prices.

Herr Schmidt bought eggs, milk, and brown mushrooms. As for the tomatoes, he was conflicted. He scolded Barbara when she bought things they had in their own garden, but it was only April, and it was questionable whether you should even eat tomatoes at all in April. Even so, he grabbed a few from the shelf and put them in his shopping basket. On a rack near the checkout, he found the current issue of the TV guide.

At the register sat a young girl with glittery eyelashes and striped talons where normal people had fingernails. She scanned Herr Schmidt's items with the tips of her fingers, until she got to the tomatoes. She asked something, but the supermarket was loud and talon-girl mumbled.

"What?" said Herr Schmidt. "Speak clearly!"

"Didnyaweighthestuff?" asked the girl.

"Do I work here?" answered Herr Schmidt. "Will I get paid to do it?"

In the past, there had been times when young cashiers broke out in tears after an exchange of words with him. Which was another reason he no longer went shopping, Barbara always got embarrassed. But glitter-girl didn't cry. She mumbled something, jumped up, gathered the tomatoes and the mushrooms from the conveyor belt, and disappeared. Herr Schmidt stood there next to his milk and eggs. He turned around, the people in line stared at him.

"What are you looking at," said Herr Schmidt, turning back to the register. The talon-fairy was already back, she had put the mushrooms and tomatoes in plastic bags and put stickers on them. He paid, she smiled and said thank you.

Herr Schmidt was stuffing his groceries into a cloth bag when he heard his name. He didn't pay any attention and instead walked out to the bicycle stand. Somebody grabbed his arm, he yanked it free.

"Walter! Schmidt, Walter! Are you deaf?"

He turned around and saw the round face of a woman, eyelids smeared with blue eyeshadow, her double chin wobbling. Why did women have to put on so much makeup. Good that Barbara wasn't like that.

"Don't you recognize me? Carola? Carola Buch?"

He'd already heard the name earlier that day.

"You did something with my photo," said Herr Schmidt. "What did you do with it?"

"What are you talking about? I don't know anything about your photos."

She wasn't smiling anymore, and had in fact taken a step back. "I just wanted to ask about Barbara. How is she?"

"Good," said Herr Schmidt.

"When will she be coming back?"

"Where?"

"You're a piece of work, Walter. Is she ill?"

"Barbara never gets sick," said Herr Schmidt. "She just needs to rest."

"I'll call her."

"That's not necessary."

With each word, she had taken another step back. Which suited him just fine.

"Say hello for me," she called. Herr Schmidt nodded and held up his hand in farewell.

The omelet was nearly like Medinski's, and Herr Schmidt realized he felt something akin to respect for the fat Polack. As a technician he valued precise instructions, they couldn't be too exact. The foamy mass waited in a buttered pan, and the tomatoes looked handsome, like something out of the dishwashing liquid advert he'd seen recently. Sebastian had made a show of thawing more pancakes. Then he tried a bit of omelet: "Mmm."

Herr Schmidt carried the plate upstairs and woke Barbara.

"What is it?" she asked.

He had put the fork up to her lips before she could even open her eyes. When she repeated the question, he deftly shoved it into her mouth. Barbara gagged momentarily, then her jaw made a few chewing motions. Herr Schmidt stood there silently triumphant.

"What is it?" Barbara said again.

"What does it taste like?" He gestured to the plate he had placed on her chest. The omelet was a little disheveled, but still cheerfully colorful. "You need to eat more, Barbara. I ran into Carola Buch while grocery shopping."

"You went grocery shopping?"

She seemed to think the eggs had just magically appeared in her kitchen. Herr Schmidt generously refrained from pointing out this logical failure on her part.

"She said to say hello from her. She's gotten fat and had only stupid things to say."

Barbara was unable to answer: She'd barely opened her mouth before he shoved in another bite of omelet. She choked. He shoved his arm behind her back and helped her sit up. He made sure she polished it all off, then handed her a glass of water.

"If you keep this up, you'll be back on your feet in no time."

* * *

The next morning Sebastian drove Barbara to the doctor. Herr Schmidt watched from behind the curtains as the boy opened the car door for his mother. It was no more than two hundred meters to Maschke's office. Herr Schmidt felt doubly unhappy: for one thing, he would have been the best person to take Barbara there. And for another, she'd left the house without breakfast, though at least she had sipped at the coffee he'd taken up to her.

Herr Schmidt waited for her return. He watched out the window, did a crossword puzzle, looked at the clock: seven minutes had elapsed. The waiting drove him crazy. He went to Barbara's computer and tapped the same button Sebastian had pushed a few days before. The screen lit up, Medinski was holding a ladle in the air.

"You're here, too," said Herr Schmidt. "Don't you have anything better to do?"

He moved the little pointer to Medinksi's midsection, as Sebastian had, and clicked. Medinski began to speak. He held green asparagus out toward Herr Schmidt and explained that, unlike white asparagus, with this kind you just snipped off the ends and didn't need to peel it to death. He really said *peel it to death*. Herr Schmidt snorted disdainfully. He could peel asparagus, he helped Barbara with it from May to June. In fact, he would go so far as to say he was markedly better at it than she was. Barbara always broke off the woody ends whereas Herr Schmidt, following instructions, snipped off just under two centimeters. She generated far more waste.

Herr Schmidt used the mouse to move the pointer around the screen. Beneath the video he found names and words. Herr Schmidt wasn't an idiot, he saw immediately that people just tossed these sentences out like in a casual conversation. The writing was a bit small, he put on his reading glasses, leaned forward, and began reading the comments line by line. Women praised Medinski's unpretentious style, while a few men men questioned individual details, they discussed different kinds of vinegar and whether chopped celery belonged in a Bolognese sauce.

Herr Schmidt thought about it, too, then after a while wondered how long he had been interested in women's things. At some stage he stood up and went to the refrigerator. Barbara always bought huge celery roots that looked like deformed heads without faces. Herr Schmidt pulled out what remained of a root from the vegetable drawer and sniffed it. The celery smelled aromatic and oddly meaty, as if it had an overly-inflated sense of self. Barbara's seemingly random selection of things she converted into food must have been more purposeful than Herr Schmidt gave her credit for. In a flash he understood there could be only one answer: celery definitely belonged in a Bolognese. This sudden revelation sent him back to the computer. He found an open field below the video and typed in this insight.

As he unhappily figured out that his contribution to the discussion had appeared under Barbara's name, the computer repeatedly made noises. Herr Schmidt soon discovered that his sentence was being rated using laughing faces and hearts.

I'm not Barbara, he added, before people got the wrong idea. *I'm her husband.*

The computer pinged excitedly. Things popped up here and there, and countless other comments began to appear below Herr Schmidt's own.

Who's Barbara?

What have you done with her?

Did you used to be Barbara? Are you trans?

I could forgive you everything, including the gender chaos, except for the celery. Celery just doesn't go in a Bolognese.

Herr Schmidt fought a rising sense of numbness.

Barbara is my wife, he wrote. *She always cooks. But she can't right now.*

Is Barbara dead? asked some asshole named Mister Superchef.

You're about to die, thought Herr Schmidt, but refrained from typing it, perhaps because, despite his clarification, he was still writing in Barbara's name and didn't know how to change that.

I want to know what else goes in a Bolognese, he typed, getting back to the subject.

I already tagged you in the video where it's explained in a detailed and idiot-proof way, wrote Mister Superchef.

I don't understand what you mean, answered Herr Schmidt politely.

I sent you a link in a DM, Barbara.

Me too, added somebody called Auguste Gusteau.

Sorry?, wrote Herr Schmidt.

My god, Barbara, put your hand on the mouse and scroll up, it's the fifth video. How ancient are you?

Hey, why are you talking to him that way, he's been nothing but polite.

Get a hold of yourselves people, we'll all be old someday.

Do you guys really believe Barbara is a man who wants to learn how to cook?

Mr. Barbara, in the menu bar above, do you see the little image that looks like a speech bubble with lightning? Click on that.

Herr Schmidt followed these directions. It made a new box pop open, with more text that explained how to prepare a Bolognese in twelve steps. He grabbed a notebook and pen and jotted down all the instructions.

Barbara and Sebastian didn't arrive back until many hours later. Herr Schmidt had looked at the clock now and then, had realized how much time had already passed, and each time felt a mercury-like chill in his chest. But fortunately the Bolognese saved him from unnecessary agony, after all it demanded his full attention. In the end, absorbed in reading the text on the box of pasta, he had in fact momentarily forgotten Barbara. There had been pasta in the cupboard, when it came to stockpiling supplies, Barbara knew her stuff. The instructions were so unambiguous that it wasn't even necessary to consult the smart-asses on the computer.

Barbara and Sebastian entered. Barbara sat down immediately, Sebastian looked around. "What happened here? Are you bleeding?"

Herr Schmidt glanced down at himself. "It's tomato sauce."

"Why don't you wear an apron?"

"You want me to look like a woman? Barbara, are you hungry?"

"Maybe later."

"You're never going to get healthy that way!"

The food had long since been ready, Herr Schmidt was getting impatient. It was disrespectful to make him wait even longer now. Sebastian seemed to notice, put plates out on the kitchen table, and they all sat down. Herr Schmidt sat in his usual spot, Barbara had leaned back and was breathing heavily, as if she had just gone for a run. Sebastian looked from one to the other, stood up, served the already cooked pasta and Herr Schmidt's Bolognese. The noodles were clumped together, you could have cut them with a knife. Herr Schmidt frowned, he had done everything according to the directions.

They ate silently, even Barbara tried a few bites and chewed pensively, as if she were trying to remember something. Herr Schmidt waited for something, a reaction, a word, at the very least a few pointers about everything he'd done wrong. At some point he couldn't hold out any longer.

"I put celery in it!"

"Not bad," said Sebastian.

"What do you mean not bad? It tastes good, it's proper food, not the crap they stuff themselves with in TV ads! Why aren't you guys saying anything? And what did Maschke say?"

Sebastian looked at Barbara, Barbara looked out the window. Herr Schmidt drummed his fingers on the table.

"Maschke sent us straight to a specialist," said Sebastian after a pause. "He called over there himself, I drove her, blood work, ultrasound, everything."

"O.K., and now what?"

"They want to admit Mama."

"What's she got?"

Barbara was still looking out the window. Sebastian waited, looking back and forth from one to the other, then shrugged his shoulders.

"It's not clear." Every word seemed difficult for him.

"Do you wish to go to the hospital, my little girl?" Herr Schmidt turned to Barbara. He'd known her for her entire life—whatever she'd done before they met was hardly even worth mentioning. He'd lived through so much with her, nothing about her could surprise him at this point. She'd been a colorless bride, blond fuzzy hair, skittish eyes. Ironically, back then she looked almost more German than he did, there was really no reason for his mother to have been so upset. To be sure, he hadn't been madly in love, but he had already learned to take responsibility, even when you didn't want to. Since then, Barbara had changed, sometimes from one day to the next, and he'd often missed these transitions. Back then there were other things that demanded his attention. He was a man, had to work. He had always worked a lot, was the king of overtime. And on weekends he had freelanced, the boss didn't need to know everything. Sometimes Herr Schmidt wouldn't recognize Barbara on the street, she'd have different color hair from one day to the next, or suddenly have a bouffant hairdo like something out of a magazine. She liked colorful clothes, he humored her. Though now and then he'd had to get a bit more strict, a bit more forceful: she'd had crazy ideas, wanted to get a job or not teach the children the German alphabet. He'd never really hit her, as fragile as she had seemed to him at first, and not even later, when she'd packed on a few pounds over the years: she never seemed as sturdy as other mothers.

According to standard measures of time, she must have become an old woman by now, but no matter how hard he scrutinized her, Herr Schmidt did not see an old woman before him. He looked at Barbara and, with annoyance, caught himself thinking she was beautiful. Her hair was thick and loosely braided, her eyes seemed to see something she would never reveal, not even to him. Especially not to him. Suddenly Herr Schmidt thought of what Sebastian had said, that he'd be able to read her correspondences on the computer now. Perhaps it wasn't a joke at all, but a warning. There were plenty of old lechers around who no longer had wives, and Barbara was perfect, he thought, taken aback. Of course there were far more old women, just based on statistics, but Herr Schmidt had seen them all: no comparison to Barbara.

"I'm not going to the hospital," said Barbara in the midst of his thoughts.

"Of course, why should you," said Herr Schmidt, sticking his fork into a clump of pasta. The difficult part of the conversation was now behind him, now they could eat in peace. "I took the herbs from your shelf, it's the French mix."

"I smell it," said Barbara. "I usually add garlic."

"Not me!" Herr Schmidt was of the opinion that he detested garlic.

"Mama," Sebastian sounded as if he had to push every word up a mountain. "Give yourself a few days, then we can talk about all of it again. Acting as if nothing is wrong is no solution."

"Leave your mother in peace. Didn't you hear what she said?"

Herr Schmidt had made a lot of Bolognese, he had to freeze more than half of it. Barbara pointed to where she kept the Tupperware containers. Herr Schmidt filled one. Sebastian had already put his travel bag in the foyer.

"Father, I just cleaned up, and now everything is covered with tomato sauce. At this rate I'll never get out of here. And for the love of god, change your clothes."

"Such insolence," said Herr Schmidt. "You always were insolent. Take the sauce for your boy."

"Thanks, but he'll be fine without it."

"Your . . . might not have made anything, this way you have dinner."

Sebastian tossed the container into his bag like a hand grenade. Good thing Herr Schmidt had sealed it up so carefully. Sebastian would probably get rid of the whole thing at the first opportunity, wouldn't put anything past him.

"What is the story with you anyway?" asked Herr Schmidt.

Sebastian mumbled something.

"I can't understand you!"

"It's not my week!" growled Sebastian.

"What?"

"Henry is at his mother's."

"Where a child belongs."

"Everyone's in agreement then. I'm off." They stood facing each other, and Sebastian started to lurch forward, but before he collided with Herr Schmidt he took a step back again and held out his hand to shake. "The fact that you're cooking is really something, Father. Honestly, I didn't make enough of it. I'm impressed. I'll call you guys. Talk to Mama, the people in hospitals aren't monsters, you know. You should never give up hope."

Herr Schmidt let go of his son's soft, girlish hand, perplexed by all these words. Sebastian stood on the threshold as if rooted there, what was he after?

"Get going." He pushed Sebastian out the door. "The boy's waiting."

"I already said it's not my week!"

"Nonsense! Everybody drives crazy on the autobahn. Don't rush."

After Sebastian had driven off, Herr Schmidt stood for a while behind the glass door. If you looked out at an angle, you could see almost the entire street, with good eyes you could even make out the license plates of cars going past. Herr Schmidt had good eyes. Mendel, on the other hand, the neighbor across the way who spent entire days doing just that, already needed glasses.

It was unbelievable how much Barbara could sleep lately. So many days went by and still she made no effort to get out of bed. Since Herr Schmidt retired, Barbara had been his timekeeper. Obviously she wasn't as precise as an actual clock. Herr Schmidt always had an eye on the time: up at five-thirty, first coffee by seven, first walk with Helmut at ten. But only with Barbara did the days fill with sound and activity, with plates and cups, with the question as to whether he would come shopping, she didn't want to carry heavy things. He grumbled but went anyway, of course. They ate lunch at twelve-thirty on the dot and talked about the weather, the garden, and the effects of the weather on the garden. While Barbara cleaned up, Herr Schmidt sat in a comfy chair in the next room, listening to her in the kitchen, utensils clattering, as he read the newspaper. He informed her how much time had elapsed since the last meal, how long it would be before afternoon coffee, then it would be dinner and he'd be able to switch on the television.

Now everything was different. He constantly had to jump-start himself. A glance at the clock no longer kept him going as long as Barbara was in bed. He had to be Barbara, for himself and for Barbara. Most of all he had to make sure she didn't starve herself to death. Sebastian had sat next to her for such a long time, incessantly whispering—what did he tell her anyway? And she him?

Herr Schmidt touched Barbara on the shoulder. She opened her eyes, they were glassy.

"Still sleepy?"

"A little."

"The boy said something about his week. What did he mean?"

"He wants Henry to spend half his time with him. She doesn't want that, she wants to move away with the child."

"What do you say? Who should be with whom?"

"Amani," said Barbara, apparently with no difficulty. "Sebastian's ex-wife."

Herr Schmidt squinted.

"I said it all along. I said that things wouldn't go well between them."

"Yes. You always told them that."

"You, too! I told you, too."

"Me, too, it's true. You told all of us. Everyone, and all the time."

"And who turns out to have been right, thank you very much?"

Barbara turned onto her other side.

"You don't want to go to the hospital, right, Barbara?"

She shook her head.

"If you don't want to, you don't have to."

She nodded. Herr Schmidt wiped the sweat from his brow, the conversation had gotten him worked up.

"You don't have to sit with me," said Barbara. He could barely hear her voice.

"What?"

"Go ahead out, go have a drink."

"A drink? It's not Thursday!"

"Ach, Walter." She smiled.

Herr Schmidt took the dog for a walk and compiled a shopping list in his head. He needed things at this point that he'd never thought about in his entire life. If he didn't keep track of them, others beat him to it and presented him with finished tasks. Sebastian, for instance, without Herr Schmidt noticing it, had deposited a bag of dry dog food in the pantry and suggested that the dog would get diarrhea from combining breakfast and dinner. It was nonsense, of course, but the bag was there now, and it had cost money. So the food had to be put to use.

In an underpass beneath the train line sat a person Herr Schmidt had never before seen. He couldn't even say for sure whether it was a man or a woman. The person wore several jackets on top of each other, feet in tattered felt slippers through the holes of which you could see wool socks. Next to the person stood what was surely a cart stolen from some grocery store, piled high with plastic bags. Helmut grew agitated, drunks frightened him. The little dog lying on a tarp next to the cart, apparently asleep, didn't stir, as if it, too, were on drugs. Herr Schmidt pulled Helmut past the pair. The sight disturbed him more than he wanted to admit. Obviously he'd seen homeless people before, but never so close to his home. He could have sworn they didn't have that sort of thing around here. After all, Barbara also often went shopping in the area, and Herr Schmidt had never needed to fear for her safety up to now.

He wasn't able to let go of these thoughts until he was seated in the Golden Stag. It wasn't Thursday, it wasn't even afternoon. The annex with the bowling alley was still closed, Herr Schmidt took a seat at a table toward the front of the place. Hanne was already standing in front of him, smiling. "Walter. I don't believe my eyes!"

She seemed to have just emerged from the kitchen, had on an apron, and had a wet dishtowel in her hands. There was not much going on at this hour, it was too early for a beer, and Herr Schmidt could make his own coffee. He could never escape the thought that Hanne's laughing, brown eyes made her look like a doe, one you wanted to reach your hand out to and tousle its brown locks. Hanne still had the round face of a girl. She looked harmless, but she was a cunning old bird. She had always been that way, and nobody knew that better than he did. When she was young, Herr Schmidt caught himself thinking for the first time about a woman's backside, more specifically Hanne's, no other. Later as well, after she'd left and returned two years later with an illegitimate brat, nothing about that body part had changed. Her Bambi-face, too, was still just as cute as it had been when she was a teenager, so nobody was surprised when the son of the pub owner married her on the spot, despite the baggage. Herr Schmidt would have taken more time to think it over had he been in that position, and in fact did so, though there really wasn't much to think about: he already had Barbara, the sight of whom gave him completely different thoughts. But there was just no getting out of it at that point.

"What'll you have, Walter? A coffee?"

"I can make coffee at home," he said, realizing he was grinning at her like an idiot—around Hanne, lots of men did. "I'll take a cider spritzer."

"At this hour?"

"That's why I said a spritzer."

She nodded and came back in record time without the dishtowel or apron, instead carrying a small round tray with a glass and a steaming cup on it. "I'll sit with you for a minute," she said. And she really did, which was always the case with her: anything she promised, she delivered.

"How's Barbara?"

"Has everyone already heard?"

"Is it a secret?"

"Nonsense. But what can I say. She just can't seem to get back on her feet."

Hanne should have said it would be alright. But she said nothing, as if she knew something that Herr Schmidt hadn't revealed to anyone yet.

"What is it?" he asked, agitated.

"You must be hungry," she said. "I'll make you a quick omelet."

He wanted to answer that he could make that himself, too. But his tongue suddenly seemed heavy, and his chin seemed to nod all by itself. Hanne disappeared again, and he sat there and stared at the pattern of the tablecloth, which repeated itself until it reached a point where there was a stain. Herr Schmidt tried to remove it with his fingernail. But it wouldn't come off, and now there was a rip in the tablecloth. The pattern was broken.

"Careful, it's hot." Hanne swung a wooden board onto the table and put the pan on top of it, filled with sizzling eggs and potatoes. "*Mahlzeit.*"

As much as Herr Schmidt liked to look at Hanne, he would have preferred to eat unobserved. She was practically consuming him with her eyes. After the first few bites he noticed how hungry he was. He made sure not to wolf it down, his throat cramped up. Was there a flicker of sympathy in Hanne's gaze?

"I cook, at home," said Herr Schmidt.

"You?" She leaned back, surprised, but not too surprised. "Well, why not. Bernd cooks at least as well as I do. Maybe better. But of course he's younger, too." Bernd was the bastard son who helped out at the pub from time to time. The pub-owner-husband was long dead, Bernd had still been young at the time of his death, and from then on he was for all intents and purposes her right-hand man.

"I'm not too good yet," said Herr Schmidt candidly. "You have to think of so much. I found a guy on the internet who explains how to do things."

"Which guy?" asked Hanne with interest.

"You don't know him. Medinski."

"Of course I know him. He has that cooking show."

"Exactly, that's the one."

The pan was empty. But Hanne had brought a basket of rye bread to the table, and there was half a slice left, which Herr Schmidt now used to mop the pan.

"The first thing Bernd ever cooked was a milk soup," said Hanne. "I still remember; I had a horrible flu, and it was his favorite dish. He was twelve. Wait, no, nine at most. Horrible stuff, but it's quick to make, and it's filling."

"How do you make it?"

"Barely worth even describing. All you need is milk and noodles—"

"Wait!" Herr Schmidt held up his hand. "Give me a pen and a piece of paper."

Milk, noodles, sugar, and salt they had at home. Herr Schmidt had insisted on Hanne describing everything in exact detail: the amounts, the temperatures. What does it mean: *Warm milk up in a pot*? At what temperature? And what about,

Don't overcook it, just warm it until it's right? Everyone considers something different to be right.

"Barbara doesn't like it too hot. Her tongue burns easily."

"Then make it the way she likes." For a moment, Hanne's smile disappeared. They'd never spoken to each other for such a long time, at least if you excluded the early years. When he was bowling with the other men, Bernd handled the bill and brought their drinks without a word. Herr Schmidt didn't care to stay for dinner because Barbara cooked better, and for another reason, as well, one he didn't want to admit even to himself. They could go ahead and call him tightfisted, which they did, a lot. Still, the omelet had been really good, and Hanne hadn't wanted any money for it. She'd made a scene of it, waving her hands, and then chasing him down as he left, stuffing the bills he had finally tucked under the ashtray—he could barely believe it—into his pants pocket.

Herr Schmidt tested the milk at least five times before it was no longer lukewarm but also not yet piping hot. He hadn't been stingy with the sugar, Barbara could do with some sugar, but surprisingly enough, it was the salt that really turned the milk and noodles into a proper meal.

"Milk soup?" asked Barbara sleepily. "Shouldn't eat that in bed, eh?"

And she did indeed leave the bedroom, with a bathrobe over her nightgown, and sat down at the kitchen table. She had difficulties with the noodles because Herr Schmidt had used spaghetti, which now kept slipping off her spoon. He gave her a knife and fork. The milk splattered in every direction as Barbara slurped up the long noodles.

"What have you done?"

"Doesn't it taste good?"

"I ate this as a child. And even back then I made a mess of myself when I did."

"You didn't have spaghetti," said Herr Schmidt.

"True, the noodles were a little different. Why do you always watch me eat?"

"I don't." Herr Schmidt conspicuously turned away, toward the kitchen counter. He saw the half-empty packet of noodles, picked it up, and put it into the cabinet. Barbara followed his movements with her eyes.

"Something wrong? Wrong cabinet or something?"

She bit her lower lip. "No. It tastes really good."

"Don't exaggerate now. It's just a bit of milk and noodles. And sugar and salt."

She leaned back and ran her hand across her stomach. The bowl was still at least half full.

"That's it?" asked Herr Schmidt with disappointment.

"It fills you up."

"Did I go to all this effort for nothing?"

The sentence slipped from his lips like a slick piece of spaghetti, and it wasn't possible to suck it back in. She looked up. It made him shudder. When she looked at him that way, he never knew what she wanted. Back when he had cursed at her, right at the beginning, when she didn't yet know how things worked, she never objected, she just looked at him exactly that way. And even then, when she did, he felt like a piece of crap and hated her for it.

"I'm going back to bed, Walter."

"Stay," said Herr Schmidt. "It's barely possible to catch a glimpse of you anymore."

He opened the door that led from the kitchen directly out to the garden. The last few days had been warm, he'd soon need to cut the lawn for the first time this year. The branches of the pear tree looked invigorated, green tips were already poking out of a few of the thicker buds. He retrieved a chaise longue from the shed, wiped off the spiderwebs: neither Barbara nor he ever used these chairs, but Karin and her best friend Mai liked to lay in the garden during their visits and to holler, "The peace and quiet here is glorious." Herr Schmidt set up the chaise, placed it in the sun, and took Barbara by the elbow. "Come on. It's warm outside. Fresh air."

Then suddenly her hand was in his. Like two children they took the five strides to the chaise together, Barbara sat down and leaned back, slightly annoyed. And now? her face seemed to ask. A light breeze tousled her hair. Barbara shuddered.

"Are you cold?" Herr Schmidt went to get a wool blanket from the house and spread it over Barbara. She grabbed it and pulled it up to her neck. "You're freezing because you don't eat and you don't move," said Herr Schmidt sternly. Then once again her hand was in his. This time he was startled. The first time he hadn't realized how dry and cool her skin was, as if it didn't belong to a living person. Barbara pulled her hand away. Herr Schmidt whistled for Helmut, who came trotting over and laid himself down obediently at Barbara's feet. With the dog added, the view was easier to bear. "What would you like to eat?" asked Herr Schmidt, still thinking of the contact with her hand.

"I'm already so full."

"That can't be. You need something nourishing. Just tell me what."

"Ach, Walter."

"I'm serious, Barbara."

He had hoped that she would say something like beef roulade and red cabbage with potato dumplings, or wild boar goulash for all he cared. He thought again about Hanne, who made a living selling food and drink and who could surely make anything, and this thought immediately annoyed him. The omelet suddenly felt heavy in his stomach, even though it had been hours since he ate it.

"Borscht," said Barbara.

"Don't be ridiculous."

"You asked."

Now she was being ungrateful. He was putting in such effort, didn't even permit himself to enjoy a pub breakfast, and she came up with this.

"You're not there anymore, Barbara."

"It's just food."

"Don't be ridiculous," repeated Herr Schmidt.

For dinner he made pan-fried potatoes with scrambled eggs, following instructions he found online. Medinski didn't have a video for it, but Herr Schmidt found an empty field on his site and typed in a query for a recipe. Answers instantly poured in. He sorted through for the halfway sensible ones, compared them to each other, and wrote down a summary on a piece of paper. Then he burned the potatoes because Karin called and he had to leave the pan to rush to the phone. Karin didn't ask about her mother, Sebastian had probably told her everything. She only wanted to know: "Everything going alright for you guys?"

"What do you mean?"

"Do you have enough to eat?"

"Stupid question," said Herr Schmidt, truthfully.

"You know you can have virtually anything delivered. I picked out a few places in your area."

"You don't need to pick anything out. We're doing fine," said Herr Schmidt. Adding, with a certain bitterness: "Your mother wants borscht."

"Oh, boy, that's really tough to make," Karin said quickly.

"That's not the problem."

"Oh, right, so you're back to being a Nazi."

"How dare you!"

"Borscht is healthy, in Berlin everyone eats it."

"You're putting me on." It wouldn't have been the first time.

"Papa, I'll send you photos."

"Of what?"

"Of people eating borscht."

The conversation was getting away from him. Then he smelled the burning potatoes and hung up without saying goodbye.

* * *

According to the calendar, it was now Thursday. How many Thursdays had he already missed? When he'd stopped in at the Golden Stag, Hanne hadn't mentioned that she hadn't seen him at the most recent bowling night. But why should she pay attention to whether he showed up or not. Maybe in the meantime the guys were meeting up somewhere else, or on a different day. Maybe they'd started playing skat as a threesome. He had just stopped going, without a word.

Herr Schmidt had nothing to hide, he would simply show up again. Barbara had no problem with it, she was sleeping when he asked her if he should go. In the days before she went to bed for what apparently was going to be a long time, he had asked her every Thursday whether he should go bowling. She had never objected, not once. Usually she was annoyed that he even asked: "Get going. As if you suddenly need my permission."

"So should I not go?"

"Go!"

He used to hope that in return she might ask him now or then whether she should go to yoga. He wouldn't have forbade her, but it would have been nice to be asked. Now he would have given anything just to have her go anywhere.

He had needed to take a few deep breaths, his hand already on the door handle, before he'd pushed open the door to the Golden Stag. The din of voices, the racket coming from the radio, the cigarette smoke clinging to the curtains, everything was the same as it ever was. He went down the long, narrow hall to the bowling alley, nodded a greeting to Bernd, who was standing at the bar. Hanne was nowhere to be seen, but he didn't want to ask for her.

The men sat at their usual table next to lane number 4. John, who was facing the door, saw Herr Schmidt immediately and nodded. Klaus shifted over to make space for him, more as a greeting than out of necessity, as there was already enough space. Quick hellos were exchanged, Herr Schmidt felt a sense of relief. But only until Günther reached over his beer and clapped Herr Schmidt on the shoulder.

"What?" asked Herr Schmidt.

"You holding up alright?"

"Have to."

"Right."

Bernd appeared with a scowl on his face, a dishtowel over his shoulder, and took Herr Schmidt's order.

"You want a puppy?" asked Klaus after Herr Schmidt had taken his first sip of cider.

"Why? Is something in the works?"

Klaus nodded grandly with pride.

"Lady? The old girl?"

"Not so old after all."

"And who's the father?"

"From up in the Taunus mountains."

"She wouldn't let Helmut in there," said Herr Schmidt, as the humiliation came welling up again.

"Nobody else, either. First time in two years. Handsome one, too. Look." Klaus reached into his pocket and showed Herr Schmidt a photo on his phone.

"Is that a proper German Shepherd? With a bloodline?" Compared to Helmut, this dog, the supposed stud, was pathetic.

Klaus swiped the screen and showed Herr Schmidt at least five photos of copulating dogs.

"Why did you take pictures of that?"

"Documentation. You see how they get along with each other? Lady's choosy."

"I'll ask Barbara about a puppy," said Herr Schmidt. That was totally preposterous: never in his entire life would he have considered taking a puppy from Lady if Helmut wasn't the father. If he were, then maybe, otherwise no way. Besides, he didn't want a new dog and Barbara really didn't, so asking her wouldn't have made any sense at all.

He shouldn't have mentioned her name.

The men all looked down at their glasses in unison, and then up again, looking past Herr Schmidt.

"Do that," said Günther hoarsely. "Go ahead and ask her. Are we going to bowl? How's your shoulder, John?"

* * *

He wouldn't have done it, not if Medinski hadn't mentioned it on his own. It was actually in a video about sauerkraut that Herr Schmidt was barely interested in. But then he spoke the hated word, and despite his Polish surname, he said it in the agreeable German way, *borschtsch*, not Barbara's way, which compressed a thousand consonants into one. At the bottom of the video, another text box popped up, and in addition to that, Medinski pointed with his finger at something else blinking to the left of his head. Herr Schmidt hated all the frantic blinking. He clicked here and there and eventually landed on a goulash that wasn't even made by Medinski; instead some Swabian housefrau had made it following Medinski's recipe, disgracefully, because she detailed at some length all the things she'd left out of Medinski's list of ingredients and what she used instead, as if everyone could just do as they pleased. Herr Schmidt tried to navigate his way back to Medinski, which, after half an hour, he was still unable to do. He had to shut down the computer along the way, but by now he had learned to restart it with no trouble at all. Luckily, afterwards, Medinski was back where he was supposed to be.

Once again Herr Schmidt found the open field and typed: *Didn't quite understand, what's the story with the borschtsch?*

He was already accustomed to the reaction. Some people already knew that despite Barbara's name he was a man and called him Mr. Barbara. It was clear to him that he made a conflicting impression, but the jeering still affected him. Only occasionally did he try to explain himself. At first he'd responded individually to every clown, explaining that he wasn't Barbara and that Barbara was laid up in bed, though he tailored it for accuracy depending on whatever the current situation was: sometimes, for instance, she was lying on a chaise longue in the garden, getting fresh air. Though he made sure not to sound distraught. Sympathy was something he welcomed even less than jokes at his expense.

Beneath his sentence, comments immediately piled up, as if people were just waiting for their cue. A half dozen know-it-alls suggested their own recipes. In a subset of comments, an intense discussion raged about whether you needed fresh cabbage, sauerkraut, or sauerkraut juice for the dish Herr Schmidt had asked about. Herr Schmidt intervened: *That's not the question. How do I start?*

One commenter tagged Medinski, after all, this was his page and occasionally he did pipe up when differences of opinion threatened to get out of hand. Someone else chimed in that Medinski was probably fed up with all the trolls and didn't monitor the comments anymore, the site was probably administered by an intern working for starvation wages.

Herr Schmidt sighed. Despite all the blather, he was none the wiser. Then a box opened along the bottom right margin and a person who introduced herself as Lydia wrote: *Barbara's husband? I can let you in on the best recipe in the world.*

It's too crazy on here, Herr Schmidt typed into the box using his right pointer finger. *Too rowdy. Can I call you?* And was surprised when a string of numbers appeared in reply to his question almost as soon as it was posted.

He went to the phone before he could think about the absurdity of what he was doing. Sebastian had been right, a hands-free headset would be helpful if you were working in the kitchen and really needed to make a call. As it was, his legs started to get stiff after three minutes while Lydia, who had answered after one ring, talked at him without periods or commas. Something about her accent reminded him of Barbara's, though Barbara didn't have one anymore, on that he would stake his life. While he said little, Lydia shouted her family recipe for the blood-red soup into his ear, increasing in volume the whole time. Her neighbors could have jotted down the recipe as well.

"Quiet," said Herr Schmidt in the middle of her explanation. He put down the phone and got himself a chair. "O.K., keep going."

At some point he had to interrupt Lydia again: he needed more precise information. It confused him terribly when she spoke of ingredients using terms like "thumb-size" and "half a glass," without first stipulating whose thumb and which type of glass she meant. With targeted follow-up questions, Herr Schmidt was able to elicit more exact instructions from her. She even gave him the names of specific brands that in her eyes made the most suitable canned tomatoes. The list of ingredients grew longer and longer.

"*Borschtsch* is not for beginners," said Lydia.

"I'm a beginner," said Herr Schmidt.

She laughed so shrilly that he began to doubt her sanity.

Once Herr Schmidt felt he'd gotten down the entire recipe, he wanted to get off the phone. He waited for an opportunity, a brief reprieve, a gap between words. But Lydia spoke without periods or commas. That was the trouble with conversations, you couldn't get out of them. Lydia had changed the subject in the meantime and asked about Barbara's condition, at which point Herr Schmidt became unresponsive. Suddenly they found themselves in a discussion of mountains, rivers, latitude and longitude.

"You're one of us, too!" said Lydia, as if this was good news, and Herr Schmidt contradicted her vehemently.

"But I can hear it in your accent!" insisted Lydia.

All of a sudden, he no longer found her likable. He mumbled a farewell and hung up.

* * *

When he was standing in the supermarket a few days later—shopping list in one hand, a clump of beets in the other—he was approached by Peter Amann. Peter was a talkative person, whose face was invariably twisted into what seemed like a slightly asymmetrical smile. As a result Herr Schmidt always thought of chronic pain when he caught sight of him. Peter's hair, following the latest trend, was combed across his bald spot, like Maschke's. Herr Schmidt, who was ordinarily not so vain, thought smugly of his own full head of hair, which he saw twice a day in the bathroom mirror while brushing his teeth. Hair and teeth, nobody could take that away from him. It's how you recognized good genes.

"You're cooking for Barbara, eh?" asked Peter, who held in his hand a pale yellow root that was unfamiliar to Herr Schmidt. "I never would have expected that of you, honestly."

Herr Schmidt couldn't believe this news, too, was apparently making the rounds. As if people had nothing better to do. He fervently hoped Peter wouldn't ask anything about Barbara.

"How is she feeling?" asked Peter with his voice dramatically lowered.

Herr Schmidt felt the by now familiar emptiness in his chest. He'd have probably done the same thing if the circumstances were reversed. If Peter's wife, Annemarie, were bedridden, he, too, as a well-bred person, would obviously have to ask about her condition as well, even if he couldn't care less. Annemarie was a friend of Barbara's, and the four of them saw each other socially now and then. Luckily not too often: unlike Barbara, Annemarie was employed outside the home, as an assistant to a manager. She had dyed yellow hair which she wore long and straight, like a little girl, and which made her tanned brown face look even darker. Herr Schmidt always thought he saw something sprinkle down from her eyelids and cheeks when she laughed too hard. Naturally the two of them had no children.

"So, how is Barbara?" Peter aimed the tip of the root at Herr Schmidt's chest.

"Ach," said Herr Schmidt.

"Not getting better, eh?" Why did Peter even ask if he already knew everything.

"You could say that."

"Annemarie is worried, doesn't talk about anything else."

"No need for that."

"We're coming by on Sunday."

"What?" The red beets slipped from Herr Schmidt's hand. "Where?"

"Your place. You seem overjoyed." Peter grinned even more broadly. He and Annemarie liked to do that whenever the four of them met at the biergarten: make fun of Herr Schmidt, because in their eyes he was both old fashioned and slow on the uptake. "Sunday at three."

"I don't know," said Herr Schmidt. "I'll ask Barbara."

"Do that." Peter waved with his root and headed for the wine section.

Making it took hours. The ingredients covered the entire

counter, a few things had fallen onto the floor. Herr Schmidt hadn't gotten around to picking them up. Reading through Lydia's directions he realized that some important details were still missing. At first he thought he'd get on the computer to ask Medinski and his vassals. But Lydia would probably feel insulted if he were to put his questions about her recipe to the whole crowd. Was he really obliged to care about that? He'd never worried about that with Barbara, though Barbara also never felt insulted, at least as far as he knew. She just wasn't the type to feel insulted. He wiped his fingertips, red from the beets, on the apron and went to the phone.

Fortunately he'd already dialed the number before he had time to consider what he would say if her husband answered. Herr Schmidt might wonder a bit if a stranger were to call out of the blue and ask for Barbara.

Lydia picked up immediately. He recognized her accent.

"Lydia? This is Schmidt, Walter. I have a question."

She seemed downright pleased to hear his voice. He interrupted her expressions of delight and asked about the correct order—did the potatoes go into the boiling water before the sauerkraut or the other way around?—and insisted on a precise cooking time.

"Ach, Walter, you're such a typical man, I've never timed it."

"Typical man? What else would I be?"

"You'll know when the potatoes get soft."

"By poking them," Herr Schmidt remembered.

"For instance."

"Can I call again later?"

"Of course. No more questions?"

"Not at the moment."

"Is Barbara doing any better?"

"Yes."

"How nice." Her voice sounded disappointed.

He went back to the battlefield and felt like a little boy. Since he'd grown up and had a family, he had always made sure not to make a fool of himself. If he was going to do something, then he'd do it expertly; if not, he would leave it to others. Now he felt like he was suddenly back in school again, facing a French vocabulary test. He wasn't stupid as a kid, could do a lot of things well: math, technical drawing, assembling things. But French stopped him in his tracks and left him standing there like an idiot. He would have constantly torn up his notebook if paper hadn't been so expensive. And besides, sticking out was strictly forbidden back then: they were newcomers, Mother had to fight. It was enough that the others made fun of his pronunciation. Despite the fact that he spoke exactly like his grandmother, and she'd always been right.

He felt like throwing all the vegetables out the window, onto the street, not into the compost, which looked and smelled proper and fresh, just the way good compost should. Mendel could go ahead and stare, the other residents could go ahead and run their cars over the parsley root.

But the groceries were innocent, they couldn't help the fact that Barbara was lying in bed. Herr Schmidt looked at the list again, then at the peeled beets, beneath whose thick skins, removed with a kitchen knife, wondrous patterning had appeared. Herr Schmidt would never have thought that vegetables could have such an elegant design. He spent eight minutes looking for a grater and then let rip.

Around midnight Herr Schmidt sat down at the computer once again, after he had turned off the flame under the bubbling, bloodred broth. He was too agitated to lie down in bed or sit in front of the television. His violet-stained fingertips, which he hadn't been able to get clean despite intensive washing, trembled at the keyboard, and the empty field on Medinski's site filled itself with unchecked spluttering. Herr Schmidt tried to delete the out-of-control letters, but it didn't work, no matter how hard he tried. He waited for immediate ridicule, but instead, worried questions piled up beneath his attempted comment.

Barbara, is that you?

Really tied one on, eh?

Don't do anything stupid, Barbara, or I'll come over.

And the smaller box opened immediately, too, and Lydia asked about how he was doing, as if she had been waiting just for this and could see into his soul through the computer.

The stupid soup isn't working, Herr Schmidt typed. *So much time wasted, for nothing. And the money I spent on all the vegetables.* He'd made a fool of himself for Barbara, at the supermarket, in the kitchen, and now he had a pot on the stove whose contents he wouldn't even feed to the dog. He'd wanted to tell Lydia privately, but he must have posted in the public comments instead. Answers streamed in from strangers.

Why start with something so difficult, Barbara?

What did you do wrong? Post the recipe.

The recipe's not the problem, Herr Schmidt tried to save Lydia's honor. *It's just not a job for a man. Barbara's in bed, and I don't know if she'll ever get up again, she doesn't want to go to the doctor, doesn't want to eat. I'm slogging it out like a kitchen maid, and all for nothing.*

Lydia asked in her message box if she could stop by, she didn't live far away and couldn't sleep anyway.

I never told you where I live, wrote Herr Schmidt suspiciously, this time, fortunately, in the right place. Lydia answered that she could tell what village it was from the area code of his landline.

It's not a village, we've been chartered as a city for 430 years!

Meanwhile, on Medinski's main page, the discussion raged on.

Try a lentil soup, my twelve-year-old son made one recently. Anybody can manage it!

Aaaaand . . . I see a food delivery in your future.

People, leave the old guy alone.

Who said he's old? Probably just a troll. How old are you, Barbara?

Herr Schmidt slammed the door to the office while they continued to make fun of him on the computer.

* * *

No wonder he slept in the next day. The man who was always up first, who made fun of people who wanted to sleep in. When Sebastian and Karin were little, he used to get them out of bed at seven on the dot, even on the weekend—*the early bird gets the worm.*

Herr Schmidt opened his eyes with a vague feeling of having experienced something embarrassing. The previous day's failure, initially a grainy image, immediately started to take on vivid color as the memory came back. He smacked his palm to his forehead and groaned. Why had he tried to indulge Barbara's silly wish. What would she have wished for next—that he learn to knit or dance? Anger welled up in him, something he hadn't felt in weeks, at least not toward Barbara. He turned onto his side, in order to tell her everything that was on the verge of spilling out of him, and then he froze.

Her half of the bed was empty.

He slowly sat up, fighting the impending dizzy spell, pulling her bedding to the side, as if Barbara might have shriveled up in the middle of the night and be hiding in the folds of the sheets. Then he felt around with his feet for his slippers. First he checked the bathroom. Not again. His heart raced for a moment. The door was ajar, he knocked, poked his head in: empty.

"Barbara!" he yelled from the stairs. "Barbara!"

"What are you yelling for?" She was down in the kitchen.

Herr Schmidt stopped on the stairs. He wasn't even sure himself why he had yelled. Barbara was at the stove. He had a good view from the doorway and had two thoughts: first, the kitchen wasn't nearly as large as he'd always believed, especially if you wanted to cook properly. He'd only realized that yesterday for the first time, when he ran out of counter space. Second, it looked bad. He stepped across the stained floor. Onion and potato peels stuck to the soles of his slippers.

"What are you doing?"

Barbara had lifted the top of the pot and sniffed. Herr Schmidt looked over her shoulder: the goop had taken on a violet tint and stared back at him with fisheye-like drops of grease. Despite the fact that he hadn't even added any meat, because he didn't have a clue how to handle it. Barbara was using a spoon to scoop out a few red-colored lumps and guide them toward her lips.

"Don't!" He pulled her hand away from her mouth. "You can't eat that."

"Let me be." She refilled the spoon, the contents of which had splashed onto the floor and both of their bathrobes as a result of Herr Schmidt's intervention, and once again guided it toward her mouth. Tasted it. But instead of grimacing, she dunked her spoon again.

"Now cut that out," snarled Herr Schmidt.

"Why are you getting so bent out of shape? It's not bad at all. Did you add salt?"

"What else should I have done?"

Barbara sprinkled some salt into her hand and then tossed it into the soup, as if she were sowing seeds. She stirred and then tried it again.

"Mmmm," she murmured.

"We'll give it to the pigs," he said. "Do you remember? I always used to want a pet pig. To fatten up and then slaughter myself."

She smiled vaguely, took a bowl, and sat down at the table after using her elbows to shove aside a bunch of kitchen utensils he'd gotten out the day before but not used. Herr Schmidt watched her with such intensity that his eyes hurt. She ate slowly but steadily, like somebody doing manual labor. What he wouldn't have given to see this a few days ago. But she just never did what she was supposed to, or, more to the point, when she was supposed to. She was defiant. When she was done, she pushed the bowl away, leaned back, and closed her eyes. Now I've poisoned her, thought Herr Schmidt. She's going to keel over in her chair and die, what a pickle I'll be in.

"Shall I take you back upstairs?" he asked. "Do you want to lie down?"

Barbara opened her eyes. "Am I in your way?"

"No sooner are you on your feet than you start talking nonsense."

He let her sit while he briefly went to the bathroom. When he returned, Barbara was standing there in her pink-splattered bathrobe trying to scrub a pan.

"What are you doing?" shouted Herr Schmidt.

"Don't shout." She swayed.

Herr Schmidt wrestled with himself. Indeed a part of him wanted nothing more than to let Barbara do it. He could take Helmut for his daily morning walk, later take out the trash, and the kitchen would once again be the way it used to be, back when he need enter it only at mealtimes. But another part of him knew this idea wasn't going to work, at least not today. Herr Schmidt took Barbara by the elbow and, with his free hand, took the sponge from her trembling fingers. "I'll take you out to the garden. You can do some knitting out there." She balked halfheartedly. His heart tensed. She could be so stubborn, and nobody knew that better than he did. But this, this was nothing. He nudged her outside, the chaise and blanket were still there, he'd forgotten to put them away. Luckily it hadn't rained.

"The borscht was the best of all, Walter."

"Don't be silly. Lie back."

She slumped into the chair. He spread the blanket over her, covering her head to foot so she didn't freeze.

"Where's your knitting, I'll bring it to you."

"Maybe later." She closed her eyes as if she'd just been lifting sacks of potatoes.

* * *

Over the next few days something akin to contentment spread through Herr Schmidt. But on Saturday he remembered that Peter and Annemarie wanted to stop by for coffee. Actually he hadn't forgotten at all, the appointment was like a spike stuck in his brain, despite the fact that he had purposefully not written it down. They had a calendar on the wall where Barbara marked the children's birthdays and those of a couple other people, as well as her hair appointments.

He needed to cancel it, but search as he might in the drawers of the telephone table, their number was nowhere to be found. So he had to ask Barbara, already suspecting she wouldn't be any help.

"Why do you want to cancel it? It'd be nice if they came by."

"Look at yourself," said Herr Schmidt, trying hard not to sound disagreeable.

"Do I look so awful?"

"You're weak."

"I'm not so weak."

"That's not how it looks."

"I'd be happy to see them."

"They'll just wear you down. They talk incessantly. And besides, there's no cake."

"Nothing in the freezer?"

He had to go look. The freezer was noticeably emptier than a few weeks earlier, as if he hadn't worked himself ragged cooking for Barbara and had instead just helped himself to things from here. Perhaps Sebastian had secretly taken things. Herr Schmidt turned over frozen packages covered in ice crystals. Then he put Helmut's leash on and headed for the bakery.

The chubby girl was sitting next to the cash register chewing gum, staring at her phone. Her hair was freshly dyed blue. He recognized her anyway, nobody else was so fat.

"Hi," she mumbled, without looking up from her phone. "Mostly sold out, but what are you after?"

With her gum, she was hard to understand, but Herr Schmidt was proud that this time he didn't have to ask her to repeat herself, as he often had to with other young people. Her voice sounded gravelly, as if she'd been shouting or had a cold.

"I need cake."

The girl shoved her phone into an apron pocket with a sigh and scanned the display case. "Sorry, not such a great selection."

Herr Schmidt lowered his head. He wouldn't have expected it to be more difficult to buy a cake than to thaw one. In the case stood a quarter of a chocolate layer cake that he had a bad feeling about just looking at. He shook his head. Next to that were two pieces of what appeared to be cheesecake with mandarin orange slices. Herr Schmidt appreciated cheesecake, but he detested mandarin oranges. He gestured to a third cake that, though the color of mud, seemed of somewhat more solid consistency.

"What's that supposed to be?"

"Whole grain."

"Don't you have any normal cake?"

"Nope," said the girl and blew a bubble with her gum. "Normal ones are already gone."

"But we're having company."

She looked at him and seemed to be waiting for something.

"I need cake. I can't always thaw things."

She frowned. "What kind do you want?"

"Something simple. Sand cake or marble cake." For a second

Herr Schmidt thought she was going to come home with him and bake him a cake. He'd pay her for it. How much could a cake cost? He looked at the labels in the display case. He hadn't realized before how much he had saved over the years from Barbara's home baking.

"It's super easy. You can make one yourself."

Herr Schmidt looked at her. She stared back at him, even stopped chewing her gum. "That kind of cake isn't any harder to make than a coffee, seriously."

"Don't be ridiculous."

"Want me to write down the ingredients?"

"Won't help."

"No, really. You just mix everything together, stir it up good, pour it into a cake pan, stick it in for forty-five minutes at 180 degrees."

"Forty-five minutes?"

"Depends on the cake pan, of course."

Herr Schmidt was already beginning to suspect it had to be more complicated. There was always something.

"What kind of cake pan you got?"

"No idea. My wife has a lot."

"Use the loaf pan. Won't stick so much. Fifty minutes."

"But before you said forty-five."

"That would be for a springform pan. But you're going to use a loaf pan." She pulled a pen from her apron pocket and ripped a piece of paper from a notepad sitting next to the register. Suddenly she was quite insistent. No young person had ever spoken to him for so long.

The shop assistant handed him a piece of paper covered with writing. She had surprisingly good handwriting, rounded little-girl letters.

"What happened to your hair?" Herr Schmidt folded the piece of paper twice and stuck it in his chest pocket.

"What's it look like?"

"No human has blue hair."

"I'm an alien. I don't belong here."

Herr Schmidt didn't know how to answer that. The girl looked at him, probably waiting for a reaction, but he just shrugged. "People will think you're crazy."

"They do anyway."

He nodded in agreement and checked to make sure the piece of paper was still in his chest pocket. Only when he arrived home did it occur to him that perhaps he should have bought a bread roll. Once again she had shared so much knowledge with him and not earned a cent for it.

Herr Schmidt noticed that Barbara was avoiding the kitchen of late. Even when she had the strength to go out and lie on the chaise longue, she went around the room she had until recently spent more time in than any other. She was also reluctant to eat in the kitchen, so Herr Schmidt had to take her plate upstairs or out to the garden, an unnecessary effort, doubly so, because he then also had to carry the virtually untouched plate back to the kitchen afterwards. Things spilled now and then. But Barbara seemed unrelenting in her sudden antipathy toward the kitchen. Despite his irritation, Herr Schmidt thought he understood the way she felt. It had been the same for him in the past. When she was busy in the kitchen, he'd never have considered sitting down in the middle of it. She didn't like it if he picked something up and left it in a different place. She had her own system. Peter and Annemarie had always given him a hard time about the fact that he didn't even help Barbara clear the table. But it had nothing to do with laziness on his part—what was so difficult about moving a few spoons from one place to another?—but rather the fact that he had never been able to do it in a way that pleased Barbara. She also had a particular idea of how to load the dishwasher, there was no point in his even trying, as she'd immediately reorganize it.

* * *

Early Sunday he pulled the sand cake out of the oven and looked around helplessly. There was no space where he could put down the hot loaf pan. He shoved the cake back in the oven, took a plastic bag out of a drawer, shoveled everything that was sitting around into the bag. There was space again. But now the full bag bothered him, he fished out the eggshells to toss them in the compost bucket, which was also full, and when he opened it a swarm of tiny fruit flies flew up. They'd never been around so early.

Herr Schmidt closed the bucket and carried it out. He had to go past Barbara, who was lying in her chaise with her eyes closed. He emptied the bucket into the compost, the rotting potato and carrot peels, eggshells—where did all this stuff come from all of a sudden—the deformed coffee filters with dried coffee grounds. Here, too, a swarm of flies came at him, and Herr Schmidt thought he could hear the critters cheering joyfully. Delicate plants were already sprouting from the sides of the compost pile, there was life everywhere, and the bottom layer consisted of rich topsoil. If Barbara filled the tomato beds with that, they'd grow so well even the Italians would be envious.

Herr Schmidt headed back into the kitchen, grabbed his dishtowel, wiped the counters. Now, finally, there really was space for the cake. He looked at it skeptically. The sand cake actually looked like a sand cake, firm and yellow. Here and there the top had clung to the pan and bits were detached like loose pieces of skin. Herr Schmidt scraped them off and then licked his fingertips. It tasted sweet. Something was missing. Herr Schmidt looked out the window to the garden. How easy it would be to ask Barbara. Instead he went to the phone and dialed Lydia's number. As usual she answered immediately.

"This is Schmidt, Walter."

"I suspected it would be."

"Do you sit next to the phone all the time?"

"No." She laughed heartily. "I carry it around with me."

"I have a question. What do you put on a sand cake to make it look good?"

"Lemon icing. Powdered sugar with a few drops of lemon juice, stir . . ."

"Too complicated," he interrupted her.

"Then just powdered sugar. You know what that is, right?"

"I'm not stupid. The whole thing will look like a snowbank then, right?"

"I don't know about that," she said. "It's too fine to be snow in my mind."

"It'll work. Goodbye." He hung up.

He'd recently glimpsed powdered sugar in one of the cabinets when he was looking for cayenne pepper, it had been in some sort of tall cannister that you had to dial the top of. Just below the opening was a sieve, and Herr Schmidt figured out why when he tried it out: the powdered sugar had a tendency to trap moisture and clump up. Contrary to Lydia's opinion, he thought the sand cake did indeed now look as if it were covered in snow. In two hours Peter and Annemarie would be here.

"What happened to you?" asked Peter when Herr Schmidt opened the door.

"Nothing," said Herr Schmidt.

Peter pointed to Herr Schmidt's chest, Annemarie stepped closer and patted at his shirt.

"Is that cocaine, Walter?"

"No, powdered sugar."

Annemarie put her fingertip in her mouth and nodded. Then she hugged Herr Schmidt and held him tight for a few moments. She had much more of a body than Barbara did. Herr Schmidt would have understood if Peter had smacked him. But he just stood there grinning while his hair, smoothed across his bald head with hair gel, glistened. He must have spent a lot of time outdoors of late, as the skin on his head already had a light sunburn.

"How are you getting on?" This was Annemarie again.

"What do you mean?"

"How are you?"

"Same as always."

He led the two of them into the garden, where Barbara was sitting up in her chaise. Herr Schmidt realized the guests needed places to sit. He brought two upholstered chairs out of the house and a folding table from the shed. It was much better to have something to do than to have to stand around idle like an idiot. Peter and Annemarie were still busy hugging and assuring Barbara with straight faces that she looked great. Finally they sat down. Herr Schmidt made his way back into the house.

"Aren't you going to join us, Walter?"

"I have a few things to do in the kitchen."

"Let's not play housefrau now, we didn't come here to eat."

"Walter baked a cake," said Barbara, and her pale cheeks gained a bit of color.

"That's what he told you. I can imagine where he really got it." Peter winked at him. Herr Schmidt turned around and went into the kitchen, so as not to speak in the wrong tone and cause Barbara to cry later. He got a knife from a drawer, turned to the cake, and suddenly felt a bit like a sucker: the powdered sugar was gone. There were just a few white spots here and there. Herr Schmidt touched the surface with his finger: nothing. He got out the sugar cannister again and made another layer of snow, made coffee, carried the coffee pot and three cups, holding them together, hanging from his pointer finger, out to the garden. Annemarie and Peter stared at him as if he were naked.

"Pinch me, honey," said Peter to Annemarie. They took the

cups and pot of coffee and arranged them on the table. Peter looked around.

"The milk," said Barbara softly.

"Don't tell me you know where the milk is kept now, Walter?"

"Cut it out!" Annemarie elbowed her husband in the ribs.

Herr Schmidt didn't care about the idiotic commentary, fetched the milk without batting an eyelash, and once again examined the cake. The powdered sugar was still there, even if the coverage wasn't as thorough. Moisture, he realized, soaked it up. Simple chemistry. He sprinkled the cake one last time and then carried it out. Barbara stared silently at the cake platter.

Herr Schmidt cut his creation into chunky slices in front of them, passed them to the guests, and then took a piece for himself. He looked at it from every angle and took a bite. The cake was a bit moist inside, but delicate, aromatic, and not too sweet. Herr Schmidt would never have said it to Barbara, but this cake tasted better than hers. It was the best sand cake he'd ever had, and the effort it took, just as the girl at the bakery had assured him, had been negligible: measure, stir, done. Did the others realize this? Herr Schmidt took a second slice and glanced at the others searchingly. Barbara still had hers in her hand and kept looking from the cake to Herr Schmidt and back again. Maybe he should have brought out plates. But he'd run to the kitchen enough times at this point.

"Much better than mine," said Barbara.

"Ridiculous." His cheeks tingled.

"There's no way you baked this," said Annemarie.

Herr Schmidt shrugged.

"He makes everything himself now," said Barbara. "And it all tastes great."

This was another lie. Herr Schmidt looked at Barbara, who had finally turned away from him and was taking tiny bites from her slice of cake. She had a tender mouth and blueish lips, as if she'd just jumped in an ice-cold lake. Unlike Annemarie, she almost never wore lipstick. She chewed slowly, pensively, slightly lost in thought.

Herr Schmidt realized for the first time that she had well-proportioned facial features. They were pretty much exactly the way they should be, not too much and not too little, though he'd never paid attention to that when they got married. When he compared Barbara's face to Annemarie's, you immediately saw the features in Annemarie's face that were too much, the too-long nose, the too-light powder that reminded him of the powdered sugar, the too-bright lipstick, and the too-yellow hair. He reached out his hand and grasped for Barbara's wrist. He could easily wrap his thumb and pointer finger around it. This revelation threw him for a loop.

Only after a while did he notice that they were all staring at him, Peter, Annemarie, and most of all Barbara, whose weak pulse he felt beneath his pointer finger. He let go. Peter looked perplexed. Annemarie blinked as if she had something in her eye. Herr Schmidt stood up.

"More cake, anyone? No? I need to pop into the kitchen for a moment."

He didn't return to the garden, there was a lot to do in the kitchen. He tried to put the things lying around back in the cabinets, and glanced out the window now and then. How could anyone talk for such a long time—and about what? What did Barbara have to tell the two of them when she'd just been lying in bed for what seemed an eternity?

When Peter and Annemarie finally left, they knocked on the kitchen door, which Herr Schmidt had closed so he could clean up in peace. Annemarie hugged him goodbye as Peter put his hand on his shoulder and made an attempt to hold Herr Schmidt's gaze for a long time, like Helmut when he wanted a treat. Herr Schmidt took the two of them to the door. Only after they were out of sight did he let out a sigh of relief.

* * *

The next day they were supposed to have bread and cold cuts for dinner. Herr Schmidt bought prepackaged salami and bologna to save himself having to exchange pleasantries at the deli counter. They had enough bread at home, even if, because of all the cooking he'd been doing, it had gone stale—but they barely ate bread anymore. He looked for gherkins for half an hour and was in a bad mood by the time he finally found the correct shelf. Who needed so many kinds, sizes, and brands? Barbara always served gherkins in a ramekin, so he didn't really know which ones he normally ate. He selected a jar that seemed vaguely familiar to him. On the way to the register he stopped in front of the shelf of sweets. Recently he'd looked in the secret drawer and realized it was rather empty. He bought the cheapest bar of milk chocolate and a roll of sandwich cookies. After all, he couldn't bake around the clock.

When he made it back home, he found Sebastian's car in the driveway. It really could have used a wash. Herr Schmidt carried the shopping bags past the car, opened the door, and listened. Barbara was in the garden, the breeze carried the sound of a child's laughter. Herr Schmidt went into the kitchen, unpacked the bags, hid the sweets in the drawer. Only then did he go out to the garden. Henry was sitting on Barbara's lap. He had grown, and Barbara was barely visible beneath him. At the sight of Herr Schmidt, he fell silent. Sebastian got up to greet him. Henry remained silent in his presence, as always, and buried his face in Barbara's chest, though he was a big boy now, he had started school this year.

"I brought cookies," said Herr Schmidt to the back of Henry's head, with its rather long, dark hair. "I had no idea you were coming, but I brought cookies anyway."

"Grandpa baked cookies for us," whispered Barbara in Henry's ear, albeit so piercingly that Herr Schmidt heard it.

"With lots of sugar and butter." This was utterly inaccurate nonsense, but Herr Schmidt didn't correct her.

"Are you hungry?" As Henry never wanted to speak to him anyway, he addressed himself to Sebastian. "You've been here more in the last few weeks than all of last year."

"That's not true." Sebastian seemed hurt again.

"Of course it's true. You must think we're going to die soon."

Herr Schmidt turned around and went into the kitchen. Somebody had to set the table. He cut bread, arranged slices of cold cuts on a large platter, and fished pickles from the jar. One fell to the floor, he bent down but wasn't able to pick it up. When he stood up again, he saw two eyes, dark like overripe cherries, peering at him through the partly open kitchen doorway.

"Come here for a moment," said Herr Schmidt. "Pick that up."

Henry came slowly toward him. He squatted down and shot back up again, gherkin in hand. Herr Schmidt picked a few dog hairs off it and popped the pickle into his mouth. He had bought the right kind, it tasted like Barbara's.

"You hungry?"

Henry shook his head.

"Why aren't you ever hungry? When I was little, I ate constantly."

Henry looked to the side. Herr Schmidt followed his gaze. The child's attention seemed to be focused on the leftover sand cake sitting on the table.

"No cake before the meal. You know that."

Henry nodded, a little too willingly for Herr Schmidt's taste. He sighed and took a large knife out of a drawer, cut a slice, and handed it to Henry.

"Take it!"

The little hand reached for the slice and touched Herr Schmidt's finger. Henry stuffed the cake into his mouth, crumbs fell to the floor, he cringed and squatted down again.

"Leave them be. Helmut will get them."

Henry stood up again, braced himself with both hands on the edge of the counter.

Herr Schmidt cleared his throat. "Grandma can't clean at the moment," he explained unnecessarily.

Henry nodded. "Won't she ever get better?" he whispered.

"Nonsense. If she eats well she'll get better. That's obvious. Right?"

Henry nodded again, looking up at Herr Schmidt, expecting more words of wisdom.

"Can you carry these plates out to the garden without dropping them?"

"I always help Mama set the table."

Herr Schmidt didn't want to comment on the parenting methods of others, especially as he was conversing so nicely with Henry, more extensively than ever before. Perhaps the boy was finally old enough that you could talk to him like a person. Perhaps Sebastian would also get there one day.

"Then go ahead. We'll need knives, as well."

They ate open-faced cold cut sandwiches on the lawn. Herr Schmidt sat at the shaky folding table, Sebastian and Henry made themselves comfortable cross-legged on a picnic blanket. Barbara, on her chaise, nibbled on her sandwich. Herr Schmidt could hardly restrain himself from ordering her to take proper bites every few minutes.

"A cold supper is completely normal. You can't expect multiple warm meals a day."

"It's all good, Father, we're not complaining in the least."

Henry peeled the meat from his bread and ate it by itself, leaving the buttered bread on the picnic blanket. Herr Schmidt couldn't bring himself to say anything because Barbara was already driving him nuts with her childish eating behavior.

"Barbara!" he finally snapped when she lowered the hand holding her barely-touched bread. It hadn't even been very loud, but Henry cringed anyway, an anxious child, no wonder, given the parents.

"What?" asked Barbara.

"Nothing." He would explain it to her later when there were no witnesses. "Give it to me," he said to Henry, who didn't understand at first that he meant the piece of bread he'd set aside. In the next instant the little fellow shrieked like a little girl because a few ants had begun to blaze a trail across the picnic blanket.

"What are you shouting for? Because of those little critters? They're living things, they're hungry, that's the way of the world. If you stop eating, you die. Caterpillars strip the trees bare, butterflies don't even have proper mouth parts. Who do you think lives longer?" Herr Schmidt chewed Henry's leftover bread; the crust was a bit slobbery.

"You ate ants," whispered Henry.

"So?"

"Did you do all the shopping yourself, Father?"

Herr Schmidt turned to Sebastian. "Why, did you bring something?"

"I mean, the salami is good, where'd you get it?"

"At the supermarket. 100 grams for 2 euros 89. You want to take some with you?"

"No, that's not what I meant."

After the food, Herr Schmidt's mood improved dramatically. He knew what he needed to do now: he would give the two of them sand cake, just as he had given it to Barbara earlier. Sebastian carried the bread basket into the kitchen behind him.

"I need a cordless telephone," said Herr Schmidt, looking for tin foil in a drawer. "I can't always run to the hall, I have so much to do in the kitchen."

Sebastian was silent for a moment, as if something were missing from this statement. Herr Schmidt waited for an answer, tired of the pregnant pauses and insinuations.

"Shall I hook it up now, after all?" asked Sebastian finally.

"What?"

"I brought you one two years ago."

"Nonsense."

"I'll show you."

They went together to the basement, past the pantry with its freezer chest and into the oblong room for which Herr Schmidt had once built shelves. On the shelves stood worn suitcases where Barbara kept non-German children's books and other useless odds and ends, hand-lettered boxes, baskets of Christmas decorations, some lamps that looked old but which Herr Schmidt could not remember ever having used.

Then there were a pile of toys, crates of colorful building blocks, large picture books, and a few packages still in wrapping paper. All of it stuff that Henry was already too old for. A boy his age should be trying to assemble a motor, experimenting with batteries and machines, but then again who cared about Herr Schmidt's opinion anyway.

Sebastian pulled an opened box off a shelf.

"Here."

Herr Schmidt couldn't understand Sebastian's triumphant look, but let it go without comment. The boy was otherwise so miserable that he should go ahead and be pleased for once.

"So it doesn't have a cord?" he asked good-naturedly.

"Didn't have one two years ago."

"And it still works?"

Sebastian rolled his eyes.

He started fiddling with the telephone jack while Herr Schmidt wrapped the rest of the cake in foil. Henry sat nearby, both hands on his knees, a chocolatey image of youth, you could have put his picture on a package of cocoa. Herr Schmidt was always astounded that this little creature supposedly had a quarter of his, that is, Herr Schmidt's, blood in his veins. You couldn't see it in him. Any sign of his kinship to Sebastian was hard to fathom, too, which is why Herr Schmidt had openly questioned Henry's parentage, even if the boy had been lighter at first. He vaguely remembered having a huge fight with Barbara, who claimed to see her own features in the face of the newborn gnome, which, given her colorless complexion, was utterly ridiculous.

"Do you get picked on a lot at school?" asked Herr Schmidt abruptly.

Henry winced. "Me?"

"Don't be stupid. *I'm* certainly not in school anymore."

Henry shook his head. "No. And I can read already."

"Are you a know-it-all? Your classmates won't like that."

"Hektor is stupid. He always kicks me. But he kicks everyone."

"You see? What would you expect from someone whose name sounds better suited for a wiener dog."

Henry smiled. He smiled so rarely that it made Herr Schmidt momentarily pause.

"There was a guy who used to bother me at your age, too," he said, suddenly hoarse. "Said things about my mother, about our family. We were newcomers. I hit him, had to go to the principal. Have you been sent there, as well?"

Henry shook his head.

Barbara fell asleep early, the visit had worn her out. She didn't want to eat anything more, either. Herr Schmidt sat around the kitchen, tired and anxious, unable to concentrate enough to do a crossword puzzle, too fidgety to go to bed. He would have liked to cook something, but he wasn't hungry. He took a quick walk with Helmut and sat down at the computer.

On Medinski's Facebook page was a new video where the chef encouraged people to use one-third celery or cauliflower when making mashed potatoes. This nonsense didn't interest Herr Schmidt, he moved the cursor around the screen and the frozen images from little film clips with thick arrows in the middle. He fought his way through the tangled mass of comments and realized to his surprise that people weren't actually friendly to Medinski, either. Sure, some praised his work to the heavens, but others called him fat or dirty and told him to go back to Poland. Herr Schmidt, who in other contexts had definitely uttered similar sentiments, felt a vein in his forehead bulge. He wanted to write something, that Medinski paid his taxes respectably, for instance, and that this shameless commenter was probably some unemployed sloth who would do better to keep his mouth shut, but then he suddenly noticed a question among all the comments: *Does anyone have a fail-safe recipe for sand cake? Mine is always too dry*. Herr Schmidt moved the mouse and clicked on the question. On cue, a blank line popped up, and he began to type. *I have one. Very easy. Wait a second.*

He retrieved the piece of notepaper with the ingredients, sat back down, and tried to find the sentence he had started his answer with, scrolling down the screen with his finger. There it was. Beneath it, other comments had already started to pile up, all sorts of people boasting about their cakes. Herr Schmidt didn't let himself get distracted, he carefully typed up what the chubby girl at the bakery had written down for him.

That's it? came instead of thanks.

What do you mean, what's missing? he answered.

I always add starch.

That's why yours is dry. Herr Schmidt leaned back, pleased with his response.

What did Barbara say about it?

He didn't know the person who posed the question, how could he remember all the unfamiliar names.

What was she supposed to say, he answered.

Did she try it?

Of course. She liked it.

Is there really a Barbara, or do you just wear women's clothes in real life?

Leave grandpa alone, you can see his profile picture is a woman.

That's why I'm asking.

Spill the beans, Barbara. Whose profile is this?

Herr Schmidt began to sweat. He moved the cursor over to the tiny photo of Barbara that showed up everywhere alongside her name, and clicked. It opened in the middle of the screen, and large enough to clearly see it was Barbara, smiling, fresh from the hair salon. Her cheeks were rounder then.

That photo is of Barbara a year ago, wrote Herr Schmidt. *She still looks basically very similar to that. A bit paler. Thinner. Doesn't eat anymore.*

Thumbs-up and heart emojis popped up next to the sentence. People went crazy. Herr Schmidt turned off the computer and went to bed.

* * *

He woke up because Helmut was howling at the doorbell as if his life depended on it. The dog was already hoarse. Herr Schmidt turned over in bed and groaned loudly when a pain hit him between the shoulder blades. Barbara lay motionless next to him. Herr Schmidt sensed the already familiar chill in his gut and expertly held his pointer finger beneath her nostrils. Barbara sneezed and pushed his hand away.

In the time it took him to find his slippers and make his way downstairs, any normal person would have accepted the futility of continuing to ring. Perhaps it was a new parcel delivery man trying to leave something for the neighbor because the old one hadn't warned him that Herr Schmidt never accepted other people's mail. In the end something would go missing and he'd be the idiot who had signed for it.

The troublemaker was now pounding on the glazed glass door. No wonder Helmut was going crazy. Herr Schmidt threw open the door: "I'm going to call the police!"

A tall grown woman with braids lurched backwards. Her flowing clothing followed her motions with a slight delay. Physics, thought Herr Schmidt, surprised as he was grazed by a piece of cloth.

"Thank god!" The woman eyed his unbuttoned pajama top. "I was getting worried."

"Do you have any idea what time it is?"

"Just after eleven."

"Nonsense."

She showed him her watch with a playful smile. It couldn't be true. He'd never slept so late in his entire life. No wonder his stomach was growling.

"I'm so sorry about Barbara," said the woman.

"What? Who are you?"

She pushed her way past him into the house. Helmut, the coward, wagged his tail excitedly.

"Walter, we know each other."

Maybe she was right. It was possible they'd seen each other before. But when and where? Sometimes he went places with Barbara, like cookouts, summer fairs, even church services. She had always talked until she was blue in the face at such events, while he stood next to her and held her handbag.

"I'm Anneke, we work together at YCC."

"What? Talk like a human being."

"She and I handle the food for the intercultural women and girls program at the Youth Culture Center."

Of course, that had to be it. Barbara and some other women baked for the neglected human trash at that concrete box near the station. She rode there every few months, balancing the baking sheets on her bike. Two or three times Herr Schmidt had driven her in the car, and they had picked up other chatty women and stowed their things in the trunk. Anneke must have been one of them.

"Barbara can't bake at the moment," said Herr Schmidt.

"I know that. I brought something for you guys."

She had a cloth tote with an anti-nuclear energy sticker on it, and she pulled something out of it that looked like a casserole dish wrapped in foil.

Herr Schmidt's nostrils flared.

"What is it?"

"Vegetable lasagna."

"Why?"

"It's vegetarian."

He pushed the bundle away. "Barbara doesn't need anything."

"You need support, too. I know what these situations are like. As a relative you take care of everything, but who takes care of you?"

"I'm not a relative. I manage to keep my wife fed."

She just wouldn't stop talking, but he stopped listening at "not to lose hope." At some stage she finally fell silent and seemed to be expecting something, perhaps a reaction from him.

"What else?"

"I could, for instance, run some errands or clean the kitchen."

"Is it messy?"

The woman said nothing. Herr Schmidt opened the front door a bit wider.

"I'll call Barbara later," she said. "If that works."

"Fine by me."

But instead of finally stepping across the threshold, she threw her arms around his neck. He gasped, patted her on the back, and stood perfectly still. It was ages before she let him go again. He stood there like an idiot, shrouded in the artificially sweet scent that seemed to saturate her clothing.

After this onslaught, he couldn't even watch as she got on her bike with all her flowing layers. He went directly to the kitchen, removed the aluminum foil from the casserole dish she'd dropped off, which turned out to be smaller than he'd thought. He hated himself for the way he chopped up and shoveled its entire contents into his mouth with a fork in the space of just a few minutes. Bits that fell to the floor, Helmut lapped up.

"It's vegetarian," said Herr Schmidt, but the stupid German Shepherd didn't seem to care.

* * *

Every time Herr Schmidt took the dog out during the next few weeks, he had the sense that he was being stared at by everyone. He tried not to stare back, but it was difficult. In every fat woman who slowly turned in his direction, like a whale, he seemed to recognize one of Barbara's acquaintances. Everywhere these partly sympathetic, partly nosy looks, the glances affecting him like touches to his skin. They all knew. Total strangers approached Helmut, who couldn't control his excitement and wagged his tail against Herr Schmidt's leg despite his disapproving hiss. Men he didn't know had the gall to place their hands on Herr Schmidt's shoulder and to offer some sort of support in something or other. And all of them, truly every last one of them, wanted Herr Schmidt to send their best to Barbara.

During one of his walks he ended up in front of the Golden Stag. The place looked closed. But Herr Schmidt turned the door handle and suddenly found himself standing in the cool, half-darkness of the cafe, suddenly barely able to see. He waited for his eyes to adjust, then pushed aside the bead curtain, got tangled up in it, and stepped forward with one strand still trailing him. He felt resistance before a sudden snap: something must have broken. Herr Schmidt approached the bar, on which sat an empty ashtray and a large ring of keys. A heavy silence filled the room. He waited a few moments, drumming his fingers on the bar, and then finally called out: "Hanne!" and then again, louder, "Hanne! Schmidt, Walter here!"

Something clanged in the kitchen, but it couldn't have been Hanne, it wasn't her kind of motion. How did he know that?

"Hanne!" he repeated sullenly.

"Coming." Suddenly Bernd stood before him, wearing an apron and wet rubber gloves on his hands. "What is it? She's not here."

Herr Schmidt looked at him, this person he'd felt sorry for when he'd been a little boy, though he was a man now, and not even a young one. How old they all must be if the children weren't even young anymore. In earlier times Bernd had been pudgy and shy, and when Herr Schmidt found his gaze lingering on Hanne's backside, the son's face would suddenly and most unwelcomely pop into his head. Herr Schmidt recalled his own conviction that nothing would ever become of the kid. This foreboding provided the surest barrier between him and Hanne. And now Bernd stood there with broad shoulders, graying at the temples, an impenetrable face.

"Where is she?"

"At the YCC."

"What's she doing there?"

Bernd shrugged his shoulders.

"The youth center by the train station, yeah?"

Bernd nodded and turned around again.

"Wait!" called Herr Schmidt, awkwardly aware of the frailty of his own voice. "Is the dishwasher running?"

Bernd looked over his shoulder. "Why wouldn't it be?"

"I always repaired it, when you were little," said Herr Schmidt. "It was my job."

"I know," said Bernd, disappearing back into the kitchen.

Herr Schmidt hadn't planned to go to the YCC. He'd never had any reason to go there, certainly didn't now, and it wasn't his problem where they got their cakes for the women's meetings now. But Helmut needed exercise. Seeing Barbara horizontal all the time hit him hard: the dog took his cues from body language and was distraught as a result.

So Herr Schmidt led him on, to the market square, along the main street. He suddenly felt like he was new in town. Back when he'd still been working for Elektro Spannert the streets and buildings had been more familiar to him. He'd been able to map them out by their various washing machines, dryers, dishwashers, and if he put a bit of thought into it, even the people who owned them. He liked the machines, any repair was more pleasurable than a sale or installation. Elektro Spannert used to stock quality things back then, you had time, nobody got upset if he took several hours to pinpoint and fix a problem in the machinery. Just getting rid of something and buying a new one wasn't yet an option. The amount of money he had saved people through his work, and where was the gratitude?

He'd arrived at the station. An S-Bahn was just pulling in, the passengers would flood the sidewalk in a moment. The homeless person had spread out in the underpass beneath the rail line. Just as a matter of course, as if it belonged to him, not the general public. His dog lay on the blanket and didn't move. Maybe it's dead, thought Herr Schmidt, this was no life for a dog, after all. A dog needed a home.

The paved yard in front of the Youth Culture Center was unusually empty, the typical smoking, chattering teens nowhere to be seen. Herr Schmidt shortened Helmut's leash, crossed the yard, and entered the concrete block through a door left ajar.

He found himself in a room with a low ceiling. Along one wall stood shelves with tattered books and board games, at the opposite end of the room was a pool table and next to it a sort of kitchenette, where a woman was emptying a dishwasher. Helmut wagged his tail enthusiastically.

"What are you doing here?" asked Hanne with her back to him.

How was it possible she recognized him without turning around?

"Your dog stinks," she answered the unasked question. "Did you get lost?"

He held Helmut's leash unnecessarily tightly, the dog howled in protest. "What was it Barbara did around here?" he answered with a question of his own.

"What?"

"Some strange woman brought a lasagna by the house."

"Anneke," said Hanne, finally turning around to face him. "She couldn't be talked out of it. Come over here." She patted the table right next to her.

Herr Schmidt ordered Helmut to sit in the corner, and made his way over to the table. As was so often the case, Hanne had on a men's shirt, jeans, and boots. Her brown hair was stuck to her forehead with sweat, and wavier than usual. Herr Schmidt squinted and looked away, following the direction she was gesturing with a wooden spoon. "You see that shift calendar? We all sign up there."

Herr Schmidt stared at the sheet of paper stuck to the refrigerator with a magnet the shape of the Eiffel Tower. The refrigerator looked familiar, but he concentrated on the sheet of paper, covered in a mess of names and dates.

"I'm signed up for today." Hanne motioned with the spoon back and forth between him and the paper. "What's it say there? Apricot sour cream cake. And where's the apricot sour cream cake? In that oven. Tastes better warm."

"Don't you have anything better to do?" asked Herr Schmidt.

"Nah." She turned her back to him again and went back to emptying the dishwasher. Herr Schmidt was in the way. She grabbed at the dishes, reached over him to put something in a cabinet, pushed him out of the way with her hip so she could open a drawer. He needed to get out of here badly. But instead he scanned the shift calendar again, deciphering the names scrawled in ballpoint pen.

"Here." Hanne pointed to a spot on the paper. "Here's Barbara's name." Herr Schmidt leaned forward. She seemed to be up in four weeks.

"What does this say? Whose chicken scratch is this?"

"Mine. It says cheesecake."

Cheesecake. He sat up straight and tried to rub the pain in his lower back but was unable to reach the spot with his hand. Barbara didn't bake cheesecake, he thought, on principle. But there it was, in black and white.

"Was she going to do that herself, the cheesecake?"

"No clue. Do you have any idea how long ago we wrote up this schedule?"

"But how do you normally do it? Does each of you get to say what kind of cake you want to bake, or is it assigned?"

"Why do you want to know that?"

"I don't want to!" Barbara was the only other person who could make him so angry.

Hanne picked up a pen and squatted down in front of the schedule.

"What are you doing?" he asked suspiciously.

"Crossing out your wife."

"Why would you do that? Leave her there."

"Now don't get upset, Walter. We'll sort it out."

"You won't sort anything out. Leave her on the schedule."

"Walter." She looked up at him. Sweaty locks, top button undone. "I'm sorry. I didn't mean it like that. Didn't mean to hurt you."

"You can't hurt me," he said slowly, carefully articulating the words. "None of you can hurt me."

Hanne stood up and wiped her hand on her pants.

"Barbara stays on the schedule," he repeated slowly. "Got it?"

"Walter. I understand everything."

"You don't understand a thing."

She bit her lower lip and averted her doe eyes. "I'm really sorry."

"Save it. Please, not you too."

As he left he nearly forgot Helmut in the corner, who whimpered worriedly behind him but didn't dare leave the spot without permission.

A small, dirty car with Berlin license plates was parked in front of their house. Helmut howled longingly. Herr Schmidt let him off the leash and the dog immediately bounded over the waist-high wall and disappeared behind the house. Karin could barely be heard because the voice of her best friend, Mai, was so much louder. It was always like that with the two of them. If there was one thing about Mai that Herr Schmidt liked, it was her loud, clear way of enunciating. Karin was the opposite, soft-spoken and indistinct like her mother.

He had to go around the house to see what was happening in his garden.

Mai was kneeling by Barbara's chaise, holding her hand. It made Herr Schmidt sick to his stomach. What was that pose supposed to be? Barbara seemed to see it the same way, she was trying to free herself, but Mai wouldn't let her take her hand away, she caressed it incessantly and described all the road construction they'd driven through. When she went places with Karin, she was the only one who drove—that filthy car was hers. Did Karin even have her own car? And where was she anyway? There she was, coming from the other side with a tray in her hand, a few glasses wobbling on it.

"Papa," she said, and her soft voice shot painfully through his body, ran down his spine, through his veins, and into his fingertips. She stopped half a meter from him, still holding the tray.

"So you ran into some traffic, eh?" asked Herr Schmidt.

Mai finally let go of Barbara. Fortunately she didn't hug him. When she hugged Barbara, Herr Schmidt worried every time that she'd break her bones. Him, on the other hand, she offered a handshake, firm like a man's, despite the fact that she was shorter than Karin.

"We've been here a while already, sitting with Mom a bit," said Karin.

"Why not," responded Herr Schmidt.

"The way you're handling things here, Walter, no, really, I have to say, hats off." That was Mai.

"Yes," said Herr Schmidt. "All according to plan."

"What are you saying, Papa? What plan? And are you thirsty?"

"Ask your mother."

"I'm supposed to ask Mama if you're thirsty?"

"Don't be an idiot!"

Karin carried the detestable tray over to Barbara's chaise. Why did everyone always have to kneel down around her.

"We have chairs," said Herr Schmidt.

"The grass is so nice and soft, Papa, we like to sit on it."

"Of course it's soft, it's watered and mowed."

"No doubt, Papa."

"Why would you say that? Who's supposed to doubt it?"

"Papa, I'll bring you a chaise so you can put your feet up, as well."

"I don't want to lie around on a chaise longue like a moron."

"We're here, take a break."

"I don't want a break!" He was getting louder.

Mai somehow managed, despite her short stature, to plant her paw on his shoulder. "What can I get for you, Walter?"

She'd called him by his first name the very first time they came to visit, years ago, and he still wasn't accustomed to it.

"I live here. You don't need to get me anything."

Herr Schmidt continued to protest, a bit more quietly at

first, then in complete silence, in his head. He didn't know himself how it happened, but at some point there was suddenly a second chaise. And he was lying on it, his feet unnaturally elevated. He had a glass of tap water in his hand. He didn't drink tap water. Herr Schmidt looked around. Karin and Mai had disappeared. Helmut, too. Barbara lay next to him on her chaise, she was squinting, her mouth twitched.

"Are you laughing at me," he asked.

She stretched her hand out and put it on his. Her fingers were light, their touch tickled. Her skin was dry again, and even thinner than before. Herr Schmidt covered them with his free hand, it was easy—she had long fingers but palms the size of a child's. A bulky wedding ring sat atop her finger, though not on his, not even for a day: he hadn't been able to stand the pressure of the metal.

Together they looked at the fence line and the neighbor's arborvitae shrubs. At Barbara's flowerbeds in front of the fence, the yellow and violet pom-pom-like flowers the name of which Herr Schmidt didn't know, but which he watered anyway. The pear tree stood in full bloom, teeming with bees.

"Tired?" asked Barbara.

For her, of all people, to ask that. Did he look tired? Probably because he was lying on this old chaise which had only been hastily freed of cobwebs. It was uncomfortable, your backside went through. And Barbara had spent days, no, weeks lying on hers. No wonder she wasn't getting better.

"I'll buy you another chaise," said Herr Schmidt. "A better one, new. Do you want something to eat?"

"Maybe later."

Karin and Mai had taken over the kitchen. Nobody had asked them to. In fact, Herr Schmidt had repeatedly asked them to let it be.

"But Papa, let us clean it up for once."

"It is clean."

"Of course, that's true, I'm not saying it isn't clean. It's just that you can't get at everything, and the floor . . ."

"What about the floor?"

"Nothing. It's all good. Just accept some help for once."

"I don't need your help."

He could say it as many times as he wanted: they turned a deaf ear, pulled things out of the cabinets, stacked them on the counters, wiped out the insides of drawers.

"I'll never find anything again! I have a system," Herr Schmidt heard himself say.

"We'll put everything right back where we found it."

He doubted that, but gave up. Not because he was weak: if he had wanted to, he could have thrown them bodily from the kitchen, from the house even. It was still his house. But he didn't want to unnecessarily agitate Barbara. She was wrong when she accused him of always picking fights with the children, saying they wouldn't want to visit anymore as a result. They obviously still wanted to come, in fact these days they visited more often and for longer periods of time than ever before. Besides, Herr Schmidt had a feeling that Karin somehow needed to do all that fussing. She could go ahead and crawl around the kitchen with a dishrag if it made her happy.

For dinner there was rice and finely-chopped, hard-to-identify vegetables, the red tint of which suggested the inclusion of tomatoes.

"What is this?" asked Herr Schmidt. The consistency didn't inspire much confidence. He could have dealt with a puree, or with large chunks that were recognizable as pieces of specific types of vegetables. But this in between thing seemed a bit off to him.

"Mostly eggplant and peppers," said Karin.

Herr Schmidt detested eggplant. He took just rice, without a word, so as not to offend anyone.

"Papa, don't be so childish. Of course you like eggplant."

"I've never eaten one in my entire life."

"That's simply not true. Ask Mama."

As if Herr Schmidt would do that.

"Is the eggplant from the garden?" he asked Karin instead.

"Too early. And besides, you never have eggplant in the garden."

"But we have peppers. Are these our peppers?"

Her silence betrayed her.

He added salt to the rice and spooned it into his mouth. Barbara had taken a thimble of eggplant and chewed it for a long time. Bet it didn't taste good to her, either. Still, he really wanted to avoid a fight. There were worse things than going to bed hungry for one night.

Mai shoveled up the goop in fine spirits. Karin was anxious again. "You know what, Papa, you can cook for us tomorrow."

"What?" Rice fell from his fork.

"Whatever you like."

"What do you mean?"

"I've heard so much about your cooking, and I'd like to finally have a taste of it myself for once."

"Don't poke fun!"

"I'm not." Tears welled up in Karin's eyes and Herr Schmidt felt a wave of guilt cresting inside him, despite the fact that he hadn't said anything wrong.

"Are you still going to be here tomorrow?"

"Papa!"

"It's okay, stop crying. I'll cook."

"We'll help you."

"God forbid. It's hard enough by myself."

* * *

He wanted something good but easy, nothing over the top. How had old Medinski put it in that one video? "People want to feel satisfied. But anyone looking for fussy frills should look elsewhere." Mashed potatoes, bratwurst, peas. The good thing about peas: you didn't need to shell them or cut them, naturally perfect, and particularly so if they came out of the freezer. This sentiment, too, came from Medinski. If Herr Schmidt hurried with his planting, he'd have his own peas from the garden in two months. And they'd be bigger than the ones from the freezer aisle at the supermarket.

Herr Schmidt looked for the cheapest ones, then for the sausages, though this time he went to the meat counter rather than heading for the prepackaged meats, as he usually did. He realized that he no longer pointed silently to the items or, as in the past, handed the butcher his shopping list written in Barbara's rounded, girlish script. Now Herr Schmidt asked questions, what was the difference between the thick sausages and the thin ones, as neither the one nor the other looked like the bratwurst Barbara usually bought. "The long ones are lamb," explained the woman, and Herr Schmidt decided instead for *leberkäse*, one slice per person and one for the pan. Barbara made the stuff once a year, although it was the best food of all. He also bought eggs.

Out at the bicycle stand, someone called his name. He packed his groceries into Barbara's basket and secured it to the bike rack, and only then did he look up. In front of him stood a woman in a blouse the color of vanilla ice cream, the only thing missing were the tiny black dots. The woman had shiny, deep-brown, nearly doll-like hair and wore a kerchief around her neck. Herr Schmidt was just about to snap at her in annoyance. Barbara's countless acquaintances were slowly beginning to get on his nerves.

"I'm Lydia."

"Who?"

He had, of course, understood immediately who she was, but wanted to gain some time.

"Lydia," she repeated, unperturbed. "Do you remember me?"

"Lydia from the computer," he said with numb lips.

"The very one." She looked him so intently in the eyes that he felt the need to take a step to the side, but the bicycle was in his way.

"You must be thinking, what is this woman doing here." Lydia trembled slightly.

"I'm thinking, how does this woman even know what I look like."

"But Walter. All the photos. On Barbara's profile page. Almost all the pictures are of you."

"I haven't seen them."

"Really? It's full of photos of you. Riding a bike, in the garden."

His cheeks felt hot. Barbara had constantly taken pictures of trees and flowers, this must have been her revenge for his getting in the way sometimes. His head began to buzz. It wasn't good that Lydia was here. The next thing you knew, somebody would see him with this strange woman. After all, everyone came here to go shopping, and everyone knew Barbara.

"Go home, Lydia," said Herr Schmidt. "Your husband must be expecting you."

"But Walter. I already told you, my husband died three years ago. Cancer." Her lipstick-red lips smiled. "The bastard," she added tenderly.

"Well, I'm leaving now. Have cooking to do."

"My husband never did any cooking."

"I never used to cook, either."

"I came all this way because of you."

Did I ask you to, thought Herr Schmidt. The conversation had reached a dead end. How could he get out of it without seeming rude?

"Buy me a cup of coffee? Please?"

Her expression reminded him of Helmut five minutes before feeding time. Herr Schmidt relented. "Fine by me. But a quick one."

The supermarket had an adjoining bakery, and in front of it stood a couple of café tables. Herr Schmidt sat with his back facing the registers at the supermarket, that way he wouldn't make it all too easy for any gawkers in line, and at the same time it allowed him to keep the parking lot and, most importantly, his bicycle in view. There was no table service. You had to order at the counter.

"Why is something like this even called a café?" Herr Schmidt pulled out his wallet and pressed a tenner into Lydia's hand. "Get yourself a coffee."

"And for you?"

"I already had one today. Get yourself a piece of cake to go with it."

Lydia headed off, the note in her hand. A few moments later she returned with two cups and two pieces of cake and placed everything on the little round table.

"Was that enough money?" Herr Schmidt reached for his wallet, but she was already handing him back a few coins in change. She sat down, painstakingly arranging the plates and cups. "I got you a piece of strawberry tart."

Herr Schmidt didn't plan to touch it. He gave Lydia exactly ten minutes. She could talk for that long about whatever she wanted to, he'd look over her shoulder and nod a few times. Then he'd go. The bill was already paid.

"How is Barbara?" asked Lydia.

"Better."

"You're such a brave, valiant man."

"You have no way of knowing that."

"I can smell it." She smiled, and he shuddered.

"Nonsense. What do you want from me?"

"Nothing. We're just chatting."

"Chatting's not my thing," came spilling out of him. His patience was wearing out more quickly than he had hoped. "I don't ask you about your husband. Why he died, and what you do with your time now that he's gone."

"I'd be happy to tell you." His outburst didn't seem to bother Lydia at all. Maybe she was accustomed to worse from her husband. "Like I said, it was cancer. So I know what you're going through. I was his caregiver to the very end."

"You don't know anything. I'm nobody's caregiver."

"Barbara is a very beautiful woman."

"That's true. But I'm not her caregiver!" Apparently she'd also looked at photos of Barbara. Herr Schmidt was overwhelmed by a terrible itch right between his shoulder blades, the exact place he was no longer able to reach.

"Do your children come over often? Take all the help you can get, Walter. Men aren't so good at that. I can stop by, too. I was my husband's caregiver, I know what you need. I can . . ."

But Herr Schmidt couldn't take it anymore. He stood up, mumbled a goodbye and rushed to the grocery laden bicycle.

Dinner was served late, after the TV news, like in Mediterranean countries. But as far as the array of foods, Herr Schmidt had no reason to be ashamed: it was simply perfect. He mashed the potatoes with half a pound of butter and worked them until his wrist hurt. He let the slices of leberkäse sizzle in the pan and then placed them on the plates, then perfectly fried surprisingly round sunny-side-up eggs, added salt, and adorned each slice of leberkäse with one of the little works of art. Karin and Mai had already set the table. Like a waiter, he served each plate individually. The three women sat there and waited to be served. But nearly as soon as the plates had been set down, Karin and Mai looked at each other and leaned almost imperceptibly closer to each other.

"It's fine." Mai's deep whisper pervaded the room.

"No, I have to address it."

"Just let it go."

"What's going on?" Herr Schmidt served himself mashed potatoes from the pot and dabbed a child's size portion onto Barbara's plate. Why did she look so embarrassed, what had he missed?

"What's up with you girls?"

"Papa, I'm sorry to have to tell you this again, especially after you've put in so much effort, but you know that we don't eat meat."

"Who is we?"

"Mai and I."

"Since when?"

"At least ten years."

"How am I supposed to know that?"

"Because I tell you every time you try to foist sausages on us."

"Nobody told me. You're adults, you can put on brave faces and eat what someone else has cooked for you."

"We don't force you to eat eggplant! It's just not . . . ," Karin paused. Mai had put her arm around her shoulders and squeezed her briefly.

"It's fine, we'll just eat the eggs and potatoes," she grumbled. "These are the most delicious mashed potatoes I've ever had, Walter! You sure didn't skimp on the butter."

"But the egg smells like leberkäse," sputtered Karin like a spoiled child.

"Give me your egg, bunnykins. Take mine. It doesn't smell at all."

They actually traded fried eggs. Karin ate in silence, her face resembling Sebastian's. Mai winked at Herr Schmidt. They were really good friends, Karin and Mai. When Mai was with her, there was less drama than usual. Karin was a pale, not particularly pretty girl, but she had a knack for making friends. Herr

Schmidt recalled a time she was rolling around with somebody on a picnic blanket in the garden, nothing but ponytails and long legs, and they were giggling so much that he had to yell at them to be quiet, as he had just laid down for a nap. Who was that again? One of the girls from the neighborhood? A school friend? He could have asked Karin, but who knew whether she'd act insulted again. It was stressful the way the children were so thin-skinned of late. Normally Sebastian was the sensitive one and Karin, by comparison, the good-natured one, the tough one.

"Berlin has ruined you," said Herr Schmidt to his daughter, but she didn't listen to him and didn't look at him, either. Instead she had turned to Barbara. "Mama!" she screamed as Herr Schmidt strained to turn toward Barbara. "Mama, what is it? Papa, hold onto her!"

Barbara came to a few minutes later; for Herr Schmidt, however, it seemed like an eternity, during which he felt divided into three different Herr Schmidts. One was frozen, a man made of stone, who felt nothing. The second cried like a little baby, while the third kept Mai from calling an ambulance. The third one asserted himself in the end.

"It'll be O.K.," Herr Schmidt repeated with numb lips. "Don't call. It'll be O.K." They'd already gotten out their mobile phones with trembling hands when he finally shouted: "Quiet!"

When it came down to it, he was still the man of the house.

Barbara lay on the TV couch, where the three of them together had carried her.

"You didn't eat any leberkäse," said Herr Schmidt once he felt she could hear him again. "No wonder your strength is flagging. Have you stopped eating meat, too?"

"I did eat, Walter. We should have that more often."

"You nibbled on a corner at most."

"It was very nourishing."

Mai pushed her way to Barbara and held a glass of water

up to her while bracing her head with her free hand. Karin took Herr Schmidt by the elbow and led him away, away from Barbara and out of the room.

"What?"

They were standing in the hallway. Mai stayed with Barbara. The deep hum of her voice, still audible at this distance, calmed Herr Schmidt's nerves like the buzz of a bumblebee.

"Papa. I understand that it's difficult."

"Nothing is difficult. Let me be."

"Papa. Your reactions are unsettling. It has to stop. We can't always be here."

"I certainly hope not."

"In all seriousness. I spoke with Sebastian, we're going to try to alternate for the next few weeks, but we do have jobs."

"What is it you want?"

"I respect the fact that Mama wishes to stay at home, come what may. I don't want to impose my will on you as far as that goes. Sebastian doesn't agree, but I understand you guys. Still, you need help if you want to see it through. There needs to be someone home at all times."

"Do you take us for little children?"

He pushed her aside, and wanted to go to Barbara. She was still on the couch, two pillows propped behind her back, her dainty hand back once again in Mai's clutches.

"Can I get to my wife?"

Mai made room. At least she wasn't debating him.

"Go out, the both of you," said Herr Schmidt.

He made sure the two of them had really left the room and called after them: "Close the door!"

Then they were finally alone, finally had some peace and quiet. He tried to lie down next to Barbara on the couch, but as petite as she was, the edge of the couch wasn't enough for him. He kneeled down next to the couch with a groan. Barbara regarded his every move with the same stoicism she showed while watching Helmut cavort in the garden. He put his hand on hers.

"How are you?"

"Better."

They looked into each other's eyes in a way they rarely did, perhaps they never had done. What was there to say when you had already said everything. Her eyes were dark blue, her eyebrows dark blonde, he reached out his hand and ran his thumb along her cheekbones. The fact that Barbara recoiled when he did made his heart sink: he had never hit her. Or had he just forgotten that he did? No, he was sure. Barbara, too, seemed to find the reflex awkward. She braced herself on his shoulder, leaned forward, and kissed him on the forehead.

Herr Schmidt wanted to say something, cleared his throat, started again. "You won't do anything stupid, right, my little girl?"

Barbara's hand still lay lightly on his shoulder.

"Don't know," she said.

* * *

Four weeks later Herr Schmidt parked the car in front of the concrete block and lifted from the trunk a baking sheet covered with a kitchen towel. He had worried that all the other women would be standing there, watching him, and that he would then drop the sheet. But nobody was there. He was, as always, early. In the kitchen of the YCC stood the only woman from that world he would recognize without any trouble even in total darkness. He'd be even less confident about recognizing Barbara. He crossed the room and set down the baking sheet. Hanne lifted the kitchen towel with two fingers and shook her head. He exploded: "What's wrong now?"

"I can't believe it," she said slowly.

"What can't you believe?"

"There's no way you baked that."

"Who else? Helmut?"

"I have a few ideas . . ." She laughed, and he remembered what it was like to want to hit a woman. Something in his face made Hanne shrink back. Hanne, who was otherwise so unshakeable.

"Walter, I'm only joking."

"I'll pick the sheet up later."

"Walter. Wait."

She laid the towel to the side and began to cut his cake into squares with a large knife. The motions were precise, quick, and somehow angry. Chop, chop, and it was all sliced up. Hanne grabbed an edge piece with her fingers and bit into it.

"Good heavens!"

"What?"

"Didn't you try it?"

For a moment he thought he'd accidentally used salt instead of sugar. He made no attempt to take a piece: the women for whom the cake was intended shouldn't go home hungry for his sake. Hanne stepped closer, so that they nearly touched, and held her piece up to his nose.

"Open up."

Suddenly he had everything in his mouth, the pastry crust, the cheese, the streusel topping. It was airy and crunchy at the same time, he tasted the butter from the crust and the vanilla from the filling. He had stuck to Barbara's age-old recipe, laboriously following her then still childlike handwriting, had been tempted time and time again to go upstairs and ask her what she had scribbled here or there and why she hadn't written more clearly. As if she could have known that he would ever be interested in it.

"Better than Barbara's," said Hanne with her mouth full.

"Don't you dare."

Hanne held out the rest of her piece to him, and it disappeared, melting on his tongue, leaving behind a diffuse taste of childhood and happiness.

"What kind of mood is she in?" asked Hanne.

As if he knew. It had been a riddle to him for his entire life, why should it be any different now. Hanne nodded, as if he'd said it aloud. Herr Schmidt liked this silent understanding even less than the idiocy of the others, who always had to quiz him and wanted to know too much. His thoughts were nobody else's business.

"She's quiet," said Herr Schmidt. They stood next to each other, leaning against the counter, and at some point Herr Schmidt realized that he was also leaning on Hanne, that he smelled the bar smoke on her clothes, which couldn't be removed with any amount of laundry detergent. Hanne's hand lay on his head, his scalp tingled. He jumped as the door was opened and a group of women in headscarves entered the YCC, chattering. He recoiled, as if he'd gotten burned by Hanne, could still feel the heat on the side of his face that had been turned to her.

Minx, he thought.

He went past the women, who recoiled from him the same way he had from Hanne, realized once outside that he had forgotten to close the trunk, checked to see whether anybody had stolen his umbrella or Helmut's blanket, which wasn't the case, and he got in. He turned the ignition and gunned the gas pedal like a teenager. His face was still burning.

* * *

The children visited constantly now. Sebastian more often, though for shorter periods of time, Karin approximately every three weeks for several days at a time. It was too often for Herr Schmidt, he had to cook nonstop, buy mountains of groceries, and constantly had to repeat that he didn't want any help with the shopping. He told the children every time that they didn't need to come so often. Sebastian responded that he personally was visiting only his mother and Herr Schmidt should just ignore him. But then Herr Schmidt caught him as he was stashing six giant packages of toilet paper in the storeroom.

He decided to act as if he hadn't noticed, after all he had to attend to the ailing tomatoes in the garden. He had stuffed the seedlings in the ground and broken a few of them, delicate work like that just wasn't manly work. Fortunately they had too many anyway. Barbara's numerous herbs hadn't blossomed yet, either, the way they should, no matter how often he watered and fertilized them.

One evening when he had adjourned to the computer and was studying the comments beneath a goulash video while Karin hung around with Barbara, Sebastian's Toyota pulled up in front of the house, unannounced as always. Herr Schmidt could see from where he was that Sebastian sat in the car a long time, rubbed his eyes, made a call, and then sat there staring straight ahead again. After at least twenty minutes, he got out. Helmut went crazy. Herr Schmidt stopped Medinski mid-sentence and went to the front door.

"Karin is here," he said as soon as Sebastian had opened the door with his own key. Perhaps the time had finally come to change the lock so the children would have to learn to ring the bell again.

"I know."

"We have a limited number of places to sleep."

"The usual warm welcome." Sebastian went past him with a plastic bag in his hand.

"What do you have there?"

"I grabbed a sandwich at the gas station."

"As if we don't have any normal food here."

"Calm down. I'll take it with me."

"That isn't fit to feed a pig."

"Fine."

Sebastian threw the bag, complete with the triangular package inside, into the trash can. Herr Schmidt took it back out and set about separating the plastic, the compost, and the actual garbage. The soggy bread and pasty cold cuts weren't even suitable for compost. The slice of tomato and the lettuce had a chance, at least after he rinsed them under the faucet to remove the pink spread.

His apprehension had been warranted: Sebastian and Karin had arranged to meet there in order to put him through the wringer. After dinner, they helped clean up and then sat down on either side of him. He could turn this way or that, but from either side came a look of reproach. Sebastian said many families in situations like this took on an East European helper. Karin mentioned two agreeable women who had just become available because the people they were caring for had both died in quick succession. Herr Schmidt wasn't stupid, he had heard about this solution, and had also wondered why he hadn't seen the two men she mentioned on the street in a while.

"That's for old people," he said.

Sebastian let out a burst of laughter only to instantly fall silent again. Karin had grazed Herr Schmidt's calf with her kick.

"Papa, the floor isn't going to vacuum itself, the bathroom looks bad after three days. You probably never noticed all that Mama used to do. Even just the laundry."

"I did laundry!"

"Four weeks ago—once."

Herr Schmidt thought it over. What had he done with the washing he'd stuffed into the washing machine back then? Had he forgotten it or had he hung it to dry? And if he had, where? Were the things still hanging? How could you simultaneously look after both the garden and the household?

"We have so many things, we don't need to do the laundry very often."

"Papa. You should hear yourself."

It wasn't that he needed to be told about cleanliness. He was Mr. Clean, always had been. At the beginning of their marriage he hadn't allowed Barbara to get away with anything. She'd been pretty messy, must have been due to her background. He had pointed out every crumb, every stain. Since then she'd become even tidier than him. He credited himself for the fact that she'd become so perfect.

"Papa, we also need to think about the time," said Karin.

"What do you mean?" He lifted his head, looked at her, his daughter, who was also slowly growing old, gray streaks in her straw-colored hair, the corners of her mouth drooping, it was difficult to get used to. Not a pretty daughter, also not a happy one, and now, it still shocked him anew every time, not even a young one anymore. "You shouldn't visit so often," he said for the umpteenth time. "Both of you. We're getting by fine."

"Please consider who you would be better able to get along with, Katarzyna or Anna. It would be a great relief to us."

"Forget it," he said. "Barbara won't tolerate a second woman in the house."

In the middle of the night, Herr Schmidt awoke. As usual, he turned to Barbara and held his hand near her nose until he was able to feel her breath on his fingertips. Relieved, he laid back and stared at the ceiling. After the fight with the children there was no way the night was going be a peaceful one. At some point Karin had buried her face in her hands despairingly, Sebastian had jumped up and run out of the room after kicking over his chair. He'd certainly inherited that temper from Herr Schmidt, at least that. Even as a child he'd had fits of rage, and although Herr Schmidt punished him severely for each one, a part of him had also been proud: these were the only moments when the boy showed intensity.

Sebastian did indeed get into his car and drive away after his emotional outburst. Then a tear-soaked Karin had glared at Herr Schmidt: "Happy now? Can you at least put up with me and Mai for a few more days?" He had shrugged.

During the night he was restless and tried to ask Barbara her opinion. She couldn't just stay out of everything and leave all the responsibility to him without ever having asked if he even wanted it that way. She had fought so hard to be able to make some decisions on her own, and the older they got, the more relaxed he was about the fact that she didn't listen to him anymore. It angered him that all of a sudden she had now stopped wanting anything at all, that he now had to puzzle over and guess about everything.

Herr Schmidt tossed and turned, checking Barbara's breathing several times. At some point he couldn't take it anymore. Helmut whined enthusiastically when he came downstairs, but the dog was sorely mistaken because the morning walk wasn't happening so much as a minute earlier than usual. Herr Schmidt went into the living room and turned on the television, kept his finger pressed on the remote until he found something that wasn't either flashing like crazy or squawking: a repeat of a Medinski show that he'd already seen, calf's liver with caramelized apples, onions, and mashed potatoes. Herr Schmidt knew immediately what he would do the next day. Barbara didn't like liver as much as he did, but he needed to think of himself once in a while. Helmut had stretched out at Herr Schmidt's feet and placed his heavy head on one of his slippers.

"Miss her, too, eh?" said Herr Schmidt.

Medinski's program was over soon, but the night went on. Herr Schmidt was wide awake, and the thought of climbing back up the stairs made his knees ache.

"You're in luck," he groaned in the dog's direction, reaching for the leash.

He hadn't noticed the way summer had crept in. The sky was cloudy, the darkness penetrated by streetlamps. The lights in the windows were nearly all out, only across the street was there a light on upstairs. Mendel was probably sitting there on his narrow mattress, alone again since his Thai wife had run away. Herr Schmidt remembered: he had never worried that Barbara would run away from him. Not because she thought he was so great—he didn't fool himself about that—but because she wouldn't have had anywhere to go. Perhaps that made up for a lot: at least she couldn't leave.

The sweet scent of linden blossoms hung in the air. In some front yards you could make out patches of withered grass despite the darkness. People acted as if the heat, which was too early and too dry, didn't affect their lawns. It did Barbara's tomatoes good, though, as long as there was somebody to water them. Herr Schmidt let Helmut off the leash. The dog trotted ahead, tail wagging, turning back repeatedly, a servile creature, hungry for love. Herr Schmidt had originally planned to take a short stroll, but his feet kept carrying him further afield.

The streets were abandoned, nobody greeted him or asked about Barbara. It was the most beautiful walk in months. He crossed the market square, where the windows of the long-closed Italian restaurant and neighboring ice cream parlor glowed a ghostly blue. The fountain was turned off, in the distance he heard an S-Bahn train. Even at this time of night the homeless person and his dog couldn't sleep undisturbed. Herr Schmidt continued on, toward a noise that suddenly rose. Soon he found himself in the vicinity of the YCC.

Helmut froze, his ears standing on edge, his body tense. The beast looked threatening if you didn't know how cowardly he really was. The dog was afraid of drunks, of people with dark skin, of umbrellas. He was particularly fearful at night.

Suddenly Herr Schmidt saw it, too: by the fence in front of the YCC two people were shoving each other, no, one was pushing, the other tugging. Helmut trembled, you could easily have taken it for a hunting instinct or bloodlust. Herr Schmidt squinted. The two people looked identical at first glance, tattered pants and oversized hoodies that raised Helmut's panic level even more. Hoodies were worse than umbrellas for him. After a few more steps the stouter of the two figures proved to be a girl. The hood slipped down, and, by the blue shimmer of her hair, Herr Schmidt recognized her as the checkout girl at the bakery.

"What's going on here?" he yelled in a jarring, raspy voice. "Leave her alone this instant!" The scuffling broke off. Two round, sallow faces turned toward him. Herr Schmidt whistled for Helmut to come to him so the dog didn't disgrace himself or—more importantly—Herr Schmidt. Though he certainly wasn't opposed to this being misinterpreted. He held the dog by the collar. The guy shoved the girl away, causing her to fall to the pavement, then ran off and disappeared into the dark.

Herr Schmidt let go of the dog, approached the girl, and held out his hand. She pulled herself up on the fence instead. "Ach, it's you."

Helmut cavorted happily, pressed his nose to her untied shoes, licked her hand, a disgrace to the entire breed.

"What would bring you here?" asked Herr Schmidt sternly.

"Why?"

"Well, you see what can happen."

She swatted the dust off her pants, which in Herr Schmidt's eyes weren't even suitable to be used as cleaning rags.

"Nothing happened."

"That guy was trying to rape you."

She laughed. "Yeah, right."

"What if I hadn't shown up?"

She continued to laugh. It was ungrateful the way she kneeled in front of Helmut and petted him, dodging his tongue.

"Your dog is super-sweet."

"Stand up. I'll take you home."

She looked at him from her crouching position. The blue hair glowed in the light of the streetlamp and made her look outlandish, more insect than human.

"Let's go. I don't have all night."

She stood up with a groan. Being overweight made young people old. She should have seen Barbara doing yoga a few months ago. As limber as a young girl.

"Where do you live?"

She pointed and they set off together in that direction: Herr Schmidt with Helmut ahead of him, her trailing. Helmut kept turning around, panting. Her gate was enervating in its inconsistency, sometimes long strides, then short quick steps.

"Is there something wrong with your feet?"

"Why?"

"You walk awkwardly."

"I walk normal."

"You don't have good shoes."

"Do you have to nitpick everything?"

She was right. Why should he care about her holey, worn-out sneakers. It's not like she sold bread with her feet. But she also breathed as irregularly as she walked, loudly, through her mouth.

"You're cold."

"Seriously?"

They cut through a little park and stopped in front of a multi-story building.

"Thanks," she mumbled.

"What?"

"This is the place. Thanks."

"Oh. Very well then."

She rummaged in her bag for her keys.

"I'm going to come in early for my bread today," said Herr Schmidt. "Wash your face before work."

"I don't work at the bakery anymore."

"What? Nonsense."

She laughed again. But at the same time a few tears ran down her cheeks. Who could understand women. Then she turned and disappeared inside. The faceless building swallowed her, as if she'd never been there.

It was four-thirty when he arrived home. Herr Schmidt didn't see any sense in going back to bed. He watered the tomatoes, which seemed to be waiting for the first rays of sun, poured a handful of food into Helmut's bowl, and made himself a coffee. Afterwards he sat down in the comfy chair, cup in hand, the crossword puzzle in his lap, and waited for the darkness outside to dissipate. The nights were slowly getting longer, he needed to be patient. He just managed to set the cup down before his chin sank to his chest.

It wasn't the first time he'd fallen asleep in the chair. It happened regularly while he listened to the radio or did a crossword. Barbara would have typically woken him up at some stage. But now he was on his own. When he awoke, his bones ached, more bones than he thought he even had. His head throbbed, as if a glowing, vibrating wire were strung from one eardrum to the other, and this wire was also somehow mysteriously connected to the doorbell. Herr Schmidt groaned and put his hands over his ears, finally some peace and quiet. Then he peeled himself from the comfy chair and set himself in motion.

The man at the door shifted from one foot to the other and didn't have any mail with him. Herr Schmidt had seen him before. But that was a long time ago, and his once young face seemed to have shriveled in some awful wrinkly way in the meantime. It was brutal when you didn't witness any of the intermediate phases. His silver hair had once been full and reddish blond, his eyes were hidden behind tinted glasses. Even back then the guy had worn glasses, which immediately made him look self-important.

"Walter." A hand reached out to him from somewhere behind a giant bouquet of flowers. "Is it an inopportune time?"

"What?"

"I called."

Not my number, thought Herr Schmidt.

"Come on in." His hand gesture was more like tossing out the garbage than an invitation.

Harald, he remembered, as he guided the guest into the dining room and offered him a seat. They'd called him Harry back then, at least when they were being nice, which was really never. Otherwise they called him four-eyes.

He laid the bouquet, wrapped in newspaper, on the table.

"They're for Barbara."

"Surely not for me," said Herr Schmidt.

Harald looked around. "Is she sleeping? I can wait."

And now? thought Herr Schmidt. Should he really send the guy upstairs to his wife, in the bedroom, in his ridiculous sneakers that looked like something Sebastian might wear, but not such an old man. Should he be allowed to sit on the edge of Barbara's bed and, like all the other guests, whisper affectedly in her ear? Barbara found it too difficult to navigate the stairs by now: when women with Tupperware containers turned up, Herr Schmidt just waved them through so he didn't have to talk to them, and the women crept up the stairs with looks of concern on their faces, working at putting on an encouraging expression by the time they made it to the top step. But four-eyes? That was all he needed.

Harald had taken up a position in the living room, standing next to the table, and didn't seem to have any intention of sitting down. Herr Schmidt left him standing there and went upstairs himself. The house shook beneath his footfalls, though it was a sturdy house, he had pitched in during construction in order to save money. Barbara lay on her side, her eyelids fluttered.

"Your admirer is here. With flowers."

She raised herself with an elbow. "Who?"

Herr Schmidt acted as if he had to think it over. Maybe a bit too long, this was getting embarrassing. "What was his name again. Harry."

"Who?" She was inept at lying.

"As if you've forgotten."

"Ach!" Barbara's blueish cheeks took on a pink hue. "Really? What's he doing here?"

She blushed deeply. His guilty conscience was gone. You're an old woman, Herr Schmidt wanted to tell her to her face, pull yourself together. He chewed over the words in his head, but Barbara was already getting up laboriously and shuffling past him on her way toward the bathroom. Pretty yourself up, Herr Schmidt wanted to call after her, it won't help you now, get dressed. His rage burned in his throat, he'd become so mild of late that he barely recognized himself anymore.

"What's with you?" Barbara had left the bathroom door open. She stood before the mirror and ran a brush through her hair, which was matted down from so much time lying down, she brushed it straight, tousled it again. Now lipstick, thought Herr Schmidt. Mascara. Anything else? What else do women put on? Perfume? She put the brush back on the shelf and turned toward him. No lipstick. Her lips were still blue. She tightened the belt of her bathrobe and tried to get past Herr Schmidt.

"Walter, let me by."

"You're going down like that?"

"What's wrong with it?"

Herr Schmidt exhaled and stepped to the side. "Nothing. Go ahead."

He watched from above as Barbara lurched slowly down the stairs. Then came the greeting, the laughing, the rustle of papers. "Aren't you silly, Harry. Just stopping by. Such a giant bouquet. What would you like to drink?" Her voice sounded almost the way it used to. Now she was waiting on him as well, though she could barely stand up otherwise. Herr Schmidt listened intently but couldn't understand what they were talking about. He went down, right past the living room, out to the garden, looking repeatedly in the window. Turned on the hose, watered Barbara's flowers a little so they wouldn't think he was eavesdropping. You could barely see inside, just their outlines. The window was partly open, but it was hopeless, no way to catch any of their conversation. He turned off the water, rubbed his hands dry on his pants, went back inside, and heard Barbara call his name.

"Now you need me?" He appeared in the doorway. They were sitting across from each other. Harry's hands on the table, Barbara's folded in her lap. Her eyes gleamed. They'd never gleamed for Herr Schmidt.

"Sit with us," she said.

"Yes, Walter, join us." Harry patted the chair next to him, as if he were the host.

"Would you like coffee?" asked Herr Schmidt hoarsely.

They did not.

Herr Schmidt didn't hold out any longer, he sat down in such a way as not to have to look directly at either one of them. His presence seemed to drain all the life out of their conversation. He turned to Harry.

"Haven't shown yourself around here for a while."

"Don't have anyone here anymore." Harry's smile was just as disarming as it used to be, back when he had futilely hoped it would spare him a beating.

"So why are you here now?"

"Had business in Frankfurt."

"It's only fifteen minutes with the S-Bahn," said Herr Schmidt.

"Exactly."

"Takes longer to drive, if there's traffic on the autobahn."

"I don't have a car."

"Why don't you have a car? I thought you were a professor."

Harry smiled. "Don't have a license."

"Seems about right," said Herr Schmidt. "Why are you kicking me, woman?"

"Walter!"

"Initially I was too nearsighted," Harry explained congenially. "I had laser surgery at some point, but by then there was no sense in getting a driver's license. You can get around just as easily without."

"But you're wearing glasses."

"Yep. And still can't see a thing."

It was just like the old days, everything bounced off of him. The flowers lay between them, colorful and heavy, as if Barbara didn't have her own flowers in the garden.

"They need to be put in water," said Herr Schmidt.

"We don't have a vase large enough," Barbara said.

"I'll go have a look."

"Come on, stay with us for a while, Walter."

"With us?" he repeated in Barbara's direction. He shoved the flowers out of the way. Barbara's hand reached out for his, and their fingers entwined. Harry watched, too, as if he'd never seen two old people holding hands before.

"And you're still teaching?" The fact that Harry was so spellbound by this gesture provided Herr Schmidt a touch of satisfaction.

"Nope. Too old."

"Don't need you anymore."

"Exactly."

"But you write books," said Barbara.

"I tell you, at this point it takes real effort for me to even follow my younger colleagues."

"Don't listen to him, Walter, he's just being modest."

Herr Schmidt wanted to let go of Barbara's hand again immediately, but she held his with a strength he wouldn't have expected of her anymore.

"I saw you recently on that talk show and barely recognized you," said Herr Schmidt. "You sounded smart."

"I'll do anything for money." As always, you never knew with Harry what was serious and what was a dumb joke.

Barbara's hand slid out of Herr Schmidt's. "I'm going to lie down again," she whispered.

"What is it?"

"Nothing. Just tired." She got up, bracing herself on the back of the chair. "I'll leave you guys alone."

Herr Schmidt hopped up awkwardly, banging his hip against the tabletop. With one hand he held onto the table, with the other he braced Barbara; Harry helped her on the other side. Fortunately the guy removed his paws again immediately. Herr Schmidt put his right arm around her waist while also using his left hand to hold her left hand. She needed her right hand on the railing. If she slips and the two of us fall in front of Harry, it's all over, thought Herr Schmidt. But they somehow made it upstairs, and he guided Barbara to the bedroom, helped her out of her bathrobe. In the time it took him to toss it over the back of a chair, she was lying down already, he just had to put the covers on her.

"What is it?"

"Just tired."

"You must be hungry."

"We just ate. Maybe later."

Herr Schmidt accepted the lie.

Harry was still sitting there as they'd left him, petting the dog. Helmut nudged the colorful sneakers with his muzzle, they seemed to annoy him, too. Herr Schmidt sat across from Harry.

"What's wrong with you?"

Harry wiped his eyes with the back of his hands. "Forgive me."

"There's nothing to forgive." Herr Schmidt smacked his knee with the flat of his hand, to call to the dog, and Helmut came over immediately. "Don't cry. You've no doubt had a great life since you left here."

"Can't complain." The guy continued to cry, though, like a little girl, and without a hint of embarrassment. The fact that he was also smiling made him look crazy.

"Everything came out alright for you in the end," said Herr Schmidt, who couldn't think of anything more consoling. "Wife, children."

"Yeah."

"How many wives?"

"Two. I'm on the second. Meredith left fifteen years ago."

"Where to?"

Harry said nothing.

"What was her name again?"

"Meredith. She was American."

"Of course."

"We have . . . had . . . a son. I mean, of course he's still alive. And now I have two stepdaughters with my second wife."

"Another American?"

"No. She's from Switzerland."

"Aha."

Harry kept sniffling. Herr Schmidt reached into his pants pocket, pulled out a checkered handkerchief, still folded, clean. Harry took it somewhat helplessly and examined it from all sides. "It's monogrammed."

"Barbara embroidered it for me. She used to have a lot of time."

Harry blew his nose directly on the monogram, then folded the handkerchief again.

"Walter," he began, then paused for what seemed an eternity.

"What?"

"I'm so sorry."

"What are you sorry for?" Herr Schmidt looked reluctantly into Harry's blue eyes, a little like Barbara's, childlike, clueless. "Ach, I don't want to know," he said.

"What don't you want to know?" asked Harry, confused.

"What you're apologizing for."

"I'm not apologizing."

"What is all this, then?"

Harry squinted, bewildered.

"Those silly postcards from all over the place," Herr Schmidt tried to jog his memory. "California. Singapore. What the hell?"

"You're right." Harry's face suddenly brightened. "I should have written more. That's what you mean, right?"

"Most certainly not."

Herr Schmidt gave up on the conversation. Now the two of them sat there silently, each with a hand on the table, the other in his lap, like mirror images, despite how different they were.

"I don't know when I'll be able to stop by again," said Harry after a while. "I'll leave you my mobile number. Please let me know immediately."

"We're doing fine," said Herr Schmidt, but Harry had already pulled out a business card and put it between Herr Schmidt's fingers. "Keep me posted, Walter, O.K.?"

"What could happen." Herr Schmidt pushed the card under the lace doily lying on the table.

"Promise me."

"Get a hold of yourself."

Harry smiled crookedly and stood up. "You haven't changed at all, Walter."

"You don't say."

"Barbara says you spend all your time taking care of things."

"You don't say."

Harry patted him awkwardly on the back. "The flowers really do need to be put in water."

"I know what to do with flowers."

Instead of slamming the door behind him, Herr Schmidt stayed in the doorway for a moment. Harry had already left their lot, turned left, on foot, peppy, not like he'd just been crying. From behind you could almost have taken him for a young man. The sun played in his silver hair. Where was he going, without a car? The station?

"Shall I drive you somewhere?" called Herr Schmidt after him, but Harry was already too far away and perhaps too deaf, as well.

* * *

Behind the bakery counter stood a young man in a white apron. Herr Schmidt frowned.

"Nope," he said. "This isn't right. Where is she?"

"Sorry?"

"Where's the chubby girl with blue hair?"

People in line behind him snorted disdainfully.

"I always bought my bread rolls from her," said Herr Schmidt without turning around to face the exasperated people.

The young man looked like Helmut, humble and devoted, probably not too bright.

"You'll have to forgive me, I'm new here."

"I see that. Where's your predecessor?" Even Herr Schmidt's saintly patience wore thin eventually.

"I can ask my boss."

"Do that."

"Can I take your order first?"

"I refuse to be served by you."

"I'm happy to be served," came a shout from the rear. Herr Schmidt turned his head and caught sight of a pair of patent leather shoes. He didn't need to know anything more.

"This is unacceptable, what you're doing," the voice added.

"Did I ask you?" Herr Schmidt was mild mannered, he even stepped to the side to put an end to patent-leather-shoe-guy's whining and let him order his cappuccino and bagel with cream cheese. The newbie sweated at the espresso machine. No way he knew to add a grain of salt. Once patent-leather-shoe-guy left, he turned unhappily to face Herr Schmidt again.

"So call him."

The young man disappeared into the back and came back a few minutes later.

"She doesn't work here anymore."

"That's not sufficient."

"I'm sorry, but I have to bake the bread rolls now."

"Was she fired?"

"I don't know."

"Did she steal something?"

The young man continued to sweat.

"Do you have her number?" Herr Schmidt waved away his own question. "Of course you don't." As he left he would like to have slammed the door, but it swung slowly and smoothly shut, making the little bell above it chime.

At home, Barbara sat at the computer. Herr Schmidt nearly yelled at her that she should keep her hands off his things. He'd forgotten that it was actually her computer. Technically the Facebook page she was in the process of reading was hers as well.

"What are you doing?" His heart raced. Could she read Lydia's messages? His questions about mashed potatoes? He felt like he was having one of those dreams where you're at the market in broad daylight without any pants on.

"What are you reading?"

She typed something.

"Who are you writing to?"

"Why didn't you respond to Medinski?" she asked him in response.

"Who?"

"Come on."

So she had read it. He leaned over her shoulder. She pointed to a box on the screen. It flickered before his eyes.

Dear Walter, what you wrote about the use of sauerkraut was quite interesting. Please send me your number, my team would like to contact you.

"Why didn't you give him your number?"

"That can't be." He leaned farther forward, her hair tickled his nose, he pressed his cheeks to her temple, where a vein pulsed. She seemed to freeze, as if he were a monster rather than her husband. He stepped back, gave her space to breathe.

"I'll give him our number, O.K.?"

"Never," he said briskly.

"He's famous, Walter."

"What's it to me."

"You're being rude."

"You don't say."

Barbara shrugged her shoulders. From this angle, sitting before the computer, she looked like a child. No wonder she was shrinking, she didn't eat anything. He put his hand on her head without thinking, the soft hair, the warm scalp. An instant later he was appalled at himself and removed his hand. But Barbara reached back for his hand and put it on her cheek. Herr Schmidt held his breath, he didn't want to do anything wrong. His fingers were too rough, had always been. Barbara's cheek was delicate. When they had first gotten together and she did something good, he would stroke her cheek as praise and mostly earned frightened looks from wide-open eyes.

"I'm going to lie down again." Without looking at him, she staggered to her feet.

"You really need to—"

"Maybe later," she interrupted.

He took her to bed and then returned to the computer, sat down on the already warm chair, and searched for the messages on her profile. Why had he never looked to see who she exchanged messages with? It just hadn't interested him—though it was entirely possible that she regularly corresponded with Harry. Certainly Harry looked like somebody who would do that. Though Herr Schmidt was no better: even now he was clicking Lydia's profile, looking at pictures of flowers and children, no doubt her grandchildren, as well as videos of military marches and male choirs who weren't singing in German.

And here was a message from some time ago that he had obviously missed. Lydia thanked him for the coffee and looked forward to meeting again. Had she lost her mind? What if Barbara had seen this? How could he tell if Barbara had read the message? He clicked again and came across the message from Medinski, that Barbara had mentioned.

My team would like to contact you.

Did I ask them to? typed Herr Schmidt. He clicked the box closed and wanted to watch a few cooking videos in peace, when the computer chimed. Medinski had answered immediately: *How's Barbara?*

What business is it of yours? Herr Schmidt's fingers were faster than his thoughts. He leaned back and felt for the first time something like regret. Medinski was an upstanding man, who worked hard and put effort into cooking sensibly and teaching others to do so. There was nothing wrong with that. Herr Schmidt tried to delete his snotty response, but only managed to expand it with a random combination of letters and punctuation marks. Now Medinksi must have thought he was nuts.

I don't know how Barbara is, Herr Schmidt typed with his pointer finger, following up the stew of punctuation marks. *She doesn't tell me.*

The answer came straight away. *What does the doctor say?*

How should I know? She went there with the children.

Didn't you ask?

We're not the type of people to constantly ask questions. She would have said something if she wanted to.

Medinski seemed to ponder his response longer this time, which unnerved Herr Schmidt.

Right, Medinski? Wouldn't she have?

How long have you been married? asked Medinski.

Forever, typed Herr Schmidt, doing the math in his head. *52 years. We had our golden anniversary two years ago.*

Congratulations, that's impressive.

I had to marry her because a child was on the way, typed Herr Schmidt. *I don't know if I would have married her otherwise, she wasn't my first choice. My mother hated her, we were newcomers ourselves, had taken a long time to gain a foothold here. In the village, you felt like an outsider for a long time, and then a wife like that, we'd fled from people like her, after all. Everything's different these days, people marry women from all over the world and nobody cares. And to be honest, Medinski, Barbara was suitable for a wife: shy, blonde. And besides, I had to. Are you married?*

For fourteen years now.

That's good. Does your wife eat well?

You could say that.

Mine doesn't eat anymore. Basically stopped. I bust my tail, go to the market, get fresh greens, this and that, but she just pokes around in it. What else should I make for her?

What does she like to eat?

Like I said, nothing anymore.

Does her mouth hurt, maybe? Does the food need to be pureed? Medinski's answers popped up faster than Herr Schmidt could send off his contributions.

What are you talking about, she's not an infant.

I used to be a cook in a nursing home, Medinski wrote, *people's tastes change with age, you need to offer soft things, spice things differently.*

This isn't a nursing home, we're normal people. Herr Schmidt searched for the exclamation point but couldn't find it. *She's just being difficult. Maybe she's taking revenge for everything I've done. In the past. I wasn't a nice guy, Medinski. She didn't say anything then, but now she's making me pay. You understand?*

Herr Schmidt waited for a reaction, his fingers on the keyboard.

You understand, Medinski?

Nothing.

Understand?

He could have spared himself the trouble, Medinski didn't answer. He'd disappeared, gone, why should Herr Schmidt's life interest him.

* * *

In front of the grim concrete block stood a bench, where an old woman with a headscarf sat. She seemed to sit here all the time, or at least when it wasn't raining. And it had only rained once of late, and then only for a short time, the summer was ignoring the annual rhythm and just refused to end. Herr Schmidt had walked past here time and time again in the last few days and had appreciated the respectful looks directed at Helmut. He sat down next to the old woman. She didn't dignify him with so much as a glance. Helmut crawled under the bench.

Herr Schmidt stayed for a long time, he had time. Lunch was already prepared, he just had to quickly cook the noodles. A newspaper or crossword would have been good about now. He stared straight ahead, at the fading lawn and a rusty swing. He'd never have let a child of his swing on a piece of equipment like that. He wondered whether he should strike up a conversation with the old woman, but she probably couldn't speak German. Normally it was the skirts who started conversations. He respected the utter lack of interest this woman took in his person.

"What are you doing here?"

He almost wouldn't have recognized her, without the apron, her hoodie over her blue hair, not even as fat as he remembered.

"I'm waiting for you."

"Huh?"

Helmut greeted the girl like an old friend. She squatted down and dared to tickle the dog extensively. Herr Schmidt decided not to beat around the bush. "I thought we had enough clothing. There were fresh piles in three dressers."

"What?"

"I also did the laundry. Two or three times. But you have to hang things up, as well. And the bed isn't made. Barbara always used to be so tidy."

"What are you talking about?"

"You're just hanging around, don't have a job. It's not good for you."

The girl stood up again, and now looked down at him from above. "What are trying to tell me?"

"I just explained." He looked up at her.

"Wait a second, did you say Barbara?"

"Barbara is my wife. She doesn't eat anymore. Well, hardly."

"Your wife is *the* Barbara?"

Why was she repeating everything? She sat down on the bench between him and the silent headscarf-woman and pulled down the cursed hoodie. "You're Barbara's husband, the one from the internet?"

"Barbara is my wife."

"You know, you're kind of famous?"

"Nonsense."

"No, really. Screenshots of your questions get shared on Facebook."

He had no idea what she wanted from him. "So are you coming or not?"

She put her hands in front of her face in mock despair. "Where?"

He took a deep breath. You had to explain things to her in baby steps, she obviously wasn't particularly quick on the uptake. On the other hand, she had been considerate to him and explained the recipes to him so he could follow them. He owed her a bit of patience.

"I'll pay you twenty euros an hour. Off the books, cash in hand."

"Twenty euros?"

"Can you clean and do laundry?" The absurdity of his plan suddenly became clear to him as he squinted and noticed the stains on her sweatshirt. Her hair looked greasy and unkempt.

"I clean like a champ," she said proudly.

"I live at Akazienstrasse 6."

"I know where you live. Everybody does."

* * *

Only on her first day working did he find out her name was Luna. Herr Schmidt had no intention of calling her this odd name.

"What were your parents thinking?"

"Call me whatever you want."

"I'll call you Heike."

"Fine by me." She looked slightly disgusted.

The question was, how was he going to tell Barbara. So he just didn't tell her at all. When she went to leave again to buy cleaning supplies and laundry detergent after inspecting the situation, Herr Schmidt handed her a key, so as not to unnecessarily draw Barbara's attention to any noise.

Barbara no longer left the bedroom, he took applesauce with cream up to her and peppered her with questions about what else she might like to have. She didn't want anything else. A week later Barbara quietly asked who the girl with the blue hair was and why she never came in to say hello. Herr Schmidt felt he'd been caught red-handed, though he had only been trying to do things correctly. He could have just invited Lydia, after all. Or Hanne. But he didn't say that to Barbara, obviously.

"You should have arranged for help a long time ago," Barbara said.

He batted his eyes, surprised.

"You told me years ago: if I died before you, you'd immediately get another woman to do the cooking," she murmured.

"Never in my life did I say that."

Barbara looked out the window, shaking her head. The leaves of the wild grapes, whose vines steadfastly tried to creep into the room, were already turning red here and there, the lawn on the other hand was still deep green, though only his lawn. The neighboring ones were yellow and dry with envy. The pears were still small and green, they probably wouldn't amount to anything this year.

"And if I were to keel over first, would you bring in Harry?" he asked.

"What are you saying? What is going on?"

"How stupid do you think I am?"

He thought he'd grown accustomed to Harry's new regular visits, the flower bouquets, the sitting around together. In fact Harry spent more time with Herr Schmidt than with Barbara, but that was only because she slept a lot even when he was visiting. Herr Schmidt thought it was fine for Harry to chat with Barbara when she was awake, but didn't like it when Harry sat by her while she slept. He waved him out of the bedroom then, gave him a beer or a piece of cake, and Harry talked about his years in America and his son in Shanghai. If you didn't stop him, it could go on forever. Herr Schmidt wondered how a man could be so chatty. Sometimes it seemed to him that Harry was alluding to Barbara with every sentence, despite the fact that she had no interest in America or China. Was he trying to blame Herr Schmidt for the fact that she had traveled so little?

While Harry talked, Herr Schmidt mostly dozed in his comfy chair. And when after a rest he opened his eyes, he would in turn find Harry sleeping.

The stream of visitors bothered him. Nearly every day somebody rang at the door. Aside from Harry, two or three other former schoolmates stopped by, though each only once, people Herr Schmidt hadn't seen since graduation, despite the fact that they still lived in the area. Heinrich, for example, who didn't get under Herr Schmidt's skin at all, even though he knew that Barbara and Heinrich had had a fling back in school. Heinrich was no Harry, though he, too, whined and cried.

* * *

Sebastian showed up, as usual, without any notice, and ran into Heike during her first week on the job. "Where'd you find her?" he asked Herr Schmidt, who was grating carrots for a rübli cake.

"On the street," answered Herr Schmidt truthfully, immediately clarifying: "She's from the bakery. Her name's Heike."

"You could have said something about her." Sebastian reached into the bowl of grated carrots with his unwashed fingers and grabbed a handful.

Herr Schmidt smacked him with the back of his hand. "It's measured out!"

"Don't be like that."

Sebastian straddled a kitchen chair and watched Herr Schmidt with his mouth hanging open. Herr Schmidt took a smaller bowl from the cabinet, grated some carrots into it, and handed it to his son. Sebastian pecked at it, Herr Schmidt couldn't look, he'd just cut a flap of skin on his pointer finger.

"Where's the boy?" he asked, holding the bloody finger under the faucet.

"At his mother's."

"What's it like?"

"What is what like? Being without your wife and child?"

"Yes."

"About what you'd expect." Sebastian licked a piece of grated carrot from his finger. "But this weekend I have him."

"You'll have to take some carrot cake for him."

"Thanks, Father, that'll make things so much better."

That evening, when the dishes were dried and back in their proper places, and Heike had gone home, Herr Schmidt sat down at the computer and wrote to Medinski. Sometimes he had the feeling that Medinski was the only one who understood him at all.

She only wants cake now, he typed. *I made her a nut cake because it's nutritious, and she ate that. Little pieces, but still. Today it's rübli, for the vitamins. Ate one and a half slices over the course of the day. Eats like a child. And it's still not proper food. I have giant zucchinis in the garden, what can I do with them?*

Medinski rarely answered, which wasn't a knock against him: Herr Schmidt respected it when people were busy. If Medinski answered, he was to the point: *What about trying zucchini cake?*

I have six different kinds of cake in the freezer because I don't want to give her the same kind all the time, so I always make new ones. I'm getting fat myself.

The thing about the freezer was a lie. Herr Schmidt didn't freeze anything. He wrapped the leftover cake in tinfoil and arranged them on the counter.

"Take this home with you," he said to Heike, who came to

the kitchen more often than was necessary to grab a bite anyway. She certainly wasn't going to lose any weight at his place.

"I still have the one from yesterday."

"Then give it to somebody else."

"You should give it away yourself. Don't you have any friends?" Everything she said sounded snotty, but she cleaned really well. A pile of clean undershirts and underpants had magically sprouted. Pantry moths no longer flew out of the cabinets and the bottoms of shoes no longer stuck to the floor. She cursed when he walked through the house with his shoes on, as if it wasn't his, and as if she were the homemaker here. He could have told her that at a certain age it was no longer enjoyable to take off your shoes. But she'd find out for herself one day.

* * *

Many Thursdays had passed with him looking at the wall calendar and suppressing a sigh. But in October came a Thursday when Herr Schmidt, without even thinking, went to the bowling alley and headed for the regular table. The other men beamed at the sight of him. They stood up one after the next to shake his hand and let him squeeze past into his regular spot against the wall. The ones who frequently needed to go the bathroom got the outside seats.

"Thought you'd disappeared."

"Nonsense. I'm always here," said Herr Schmidt jokingly.

"Forgot what you look like."

"I only missed one week."

"He can't count anymore either."

"What, do you take attendance now?" He sat down. "You've all gotten old."

"And you've gotten fat."

"What else is new?" He looked at their smiling faces. Was it possible they'd missed him a little?

The last few times he'd been there, the previous winter, when he didn't have to think about Barbara the whole time, they had reserved and paid for a lane but none of the other three had actually picked up a ball. John had for months had something wrong with his shoulder, which they'd ridiculed as a poor excuse, but out of solidarity most of them hadn't bowled. Only Herr Schmidt blithely rolled one strike after the next. He remembered how once when a final pin had remained upright and he'd watched it teetering, he saw himself in that last pin standing, until it finally fell over.

Herr Schmidt feared the men's silence, but he feared questions even more. He remembered sitting together at this table just a few days after the death of Klaus's wife, silent, for an hour. The funeral had been horrible, Herr Schmidt in the back row, not wanting to press forward as the others did, Barbara crying at his side. He had barred her from taking Klaus homemade food, said Klaus would let them know if he needed anything, he was a grown man after all. And sure enough, Klaus had affirmed that he didn't need anything, he had the Polish woman who had taken care of his wife to the end. The week after the funeral he came bowling, though he had sat blankly staring at his beer and not reacted when addressed. "You need to shave when you go out," Günther had told Klaus. Günther was fashionable, always had been, even as a young man, leather jacket, hair gel. Two weeks later Klaus was clean-shaven, wearing a freshly laundered shirt, and actually participated again, bowling with merciless precision. The Polish woman was still with him. Sometimes you saw them together at the shops. Local people said he should have moved away with her.

Bernd brought over the cider spritzers and banged the mugs down on the table in front of Herr Schmidt.

"He can't stand me," said Herr Schmidt, wiping splashed cider from his sleeve. "What did I ever do to him?"

"As if you don't know," said Klaus.

"I never did anything to him."

"Not directly," said Günther.

"I never did anything to anyone."

"Take it easy."

"I never promised Hanne anything. I had Barbara."

Deep inside he felt a tingle of satisfaction. Hanne didn't belong to anyone. She was a trophy, not his, maybe, but it still gave him a sense of pride that she could have been. But instead of being permitted to savor that tingle, he had to watch as the men slumped when Barbara's name came up, as their eyes went dim, as if somebody had turned off the lights behind them.

"Barbara's doing well," Herr Schmidt said clearly and distinctly.

They said nothing.

"I bake cakes now like a woman. She even likes them."

They feigned silent admiration.

"Chocolate cake, apple cake." He dug his hole deeper and deeper. "Nice and moist, I never let it get hard or dry. The pears will be ripe soon. She chews so slowly you'd think her mouth hurt."

Klaus stared at his hands. The other two managed to hold their gaze on Herr Schmidt.

"The most important thing is that she doesn't starve. I make sure of that. Also don't want her to have to be fed with an IV or something. That's no way to live."

"I had an IV once," said Günther. "Wasn't so bad."

As if he didn't really understand.

"Anyway," said Herr Schmidt. "Let's have a look at Lady's puppies, Klaus."

He watched as the light behind the men's eyes came back on, how their shoulders relaxed, how their eyelids defied gravity once again. How similar they all looked, whether bald or still well-appointed, like Herr Schmidt. They all made the same facial expression as the chimpanzee Herr Schmidt had seen years ago at the zoo with the children. Sitting behind a pane of glass, the beast had made eye contact with him for a fraction of a second and thereby so thoroughly mortified Herr Schmidt that he never again took the children to the zoo.

Herr Schmidt was freezing on the way home. Normally Barbara was the one who was cold. He didn't typically notice such things. Now he missed his cardigan, and he envisioned himself putting it on as soon as he got home. Perhaps they'd need to put the heating on earlier this year, for Barbara's sake, as she didn't move at all.

Herr Schmidt put his bicycle in the garage, right next to Barbara's. He checked the air in Barbara's tires and got out the pump.

When he went inside, the lights were already on. Heike was checking herself in the mirror, preparing to leave, hood over her head, headphones already in her ears. On the side table sat cards, stone hearts, and angel figurines that Barbara's visitors had brought her for the purpose of encouragement. Herr Schmidt first looked in the office, then the bedroom. "Have you seen my cardigan?" he asked Barbara, whose eyelids fluttered. Maybe she was really asleep. He checked to make sure she was breathing, pulled up her covers, and broke off a tiny piece of the cake he had left on her bedside table. He pushed the crumb between her lips. A weak swallowing motion reassured him. He didn't want to force down any more, and ate the rest himself. Tasted good.

The pear tree looked pretty even in the milky darkness, the little yellowish fruits glimmered between the leaves whose green coloration was slowly losing its lusciousness. "We're still sitting here in November," said Herr Schmidt. "But at some point enough is enough, Barbara. What do you think?"

He held Barbara's hand, which disappeared in his, and ran

his coarse fingers over the bones of hers. The branches of the pear tree drooped. So many pears, how many cakes would they make? As far as he remembered, the fruit didn't keep, quickly got bruises and rotted.

"Lady's puppies are already getting big, the little varmints. You have to see them. Do you want to turn onto your other side?" Barbara was asleep.

* * *

"Christmas," said Klaus after the second round.

"Where?"

"Here." Klaus pointed at a few evergreen boughs in a vase. "And there." Above the bar hung a gleaming yellow tinsel garland.

"Ach, quit acting like that," mumbled John. "Hanne always decorates the place for the first day of advent."

"And what Sunday of advent is it today?"

"It's not. It's only Thursday."

"Shitty stuff," said Herr Schmidt.

"Don't talk about it that way. He's always listening."

"Who?"

"*Him.*" Klaus glanced up at the ceiling.

"He can kiss my ass. Shitty stuff!"

"Things will be alright, Walter. It'll be over eventually."

"No," said Herr Schmidt. "I don't want it to be over."

Christmas was not a topic for the group of regulars. Herr Schmidt had recently harvested the pears, after long waiting in vain for them to turn yellow and fall on their own. Every year the tree just did what it wanted. The pears were green and hard, he had put them in a wooden crate and now checked them every morning to see if they'd ripened.

Christmas was a holiday for women and children. Barbara always wrapped a string of lights around the rubber tree in the TV room and hung another in the garden hedge. Waste of electricity, but what could he do. Other women were worse, most of the houses on their street had angels peering out of the windows, lights blinking frenetically in the front yard, and some eaves had stunted but frighteningly realistic Santas hanging from them. Herr Schmidt always had to think of the time he once climbed up to the balcony of the sister dormitory: they'd ridden their bikes to the local hospital, seventeen kilometers. The girls' happy shrieks. He looked good back then, blond, muscular. A few of them had crushes on him. But none was as gentle as Barbara, who couldn't say no, even when it was to her detriment. To this day he hadn't figured out whether she'd been particularly in love or particularly weak. Was there even a difference?

He forced himself to think about Christmas again. People let the holiday drive them crazy weeks, no, months in advance. Karin and Sebastian became more uncommunicative, some couples stopped by, "to see Barbara one more time." Even Mendel and his mother had rung the doorbell and dropped off a bag of chocolate nuts. To Herr Schmidt, there seemed to be a certain impatience to their questions about Barbara's condition.

* * *

"Shall I bake Christmas cookies, too?" he asked the men the following week.

"You can buy them, Walter," said John.

"What do you take me for?"

The awkwardness of the others was what bothered him the most. These Thursday afternoons were supposed to be a hiatus, from wives, from headaches, from topics that made your heart skip a beat. Just bowling, German Shepherds, pruning fruit trees. He had the rest of the week for provocation and aggravation.

"If you need anything, Walter . . ."

"I need my wife."

Their faces wore him down.

"Why does everyone think they know better," Herr Schmidt exploded. "Every idiot on the street has an opinion that counts more than mine. Is she your wife? Are any of them there, day and night, every goddamned second? Other than me, Heike is there the most, but at least she doesn't meddle in my business. I'm telling you: Barbara isn't dying."

"Walter." John put a hand on his shoulder and then took it away immediately. "We know all the diagnoses."

"You don't know shit!" His vision began to blur, he coughed into his sleeve, that was the only thing missing now, for him to get weak, too. "I'll get her back on her feet. I'm telling you."

They cleared their throats, wiped their noses on their napkins.

"What's going on here?" Hanne was suddenly standing behind them, tray in hand. He'd probably yelled louder than was permitted; she paid attention to such things, ever since somebody had been stabbed here decades ago.

"Walter's being difficult."

"That's the way he is." She pushed him aside with her hips, sat down next to him on the bench, casually cozied her thigh up against his. The men watched it all. Minx, he thought. The palms of his hands itched. "It's on the house," said Hanne, refilling their glasses. She had added a fifth, for herself. The men looked as if they couldn't believe their luck. Herr Schmidt, though, boiled with rage.

* * *

The children wanted to talk about Christmas with him. First they only made hints—"Once again it looks like there won't be a white Christmas"—then they got pushier: "The neighbors already have garlands up." When Sebastian arranged a row of gift-wrapped presents on the windowsill, Herr Schmidt barked: "What is that shit? I don't give a damn about Christmas."

"It's not for you, it's for the housekeeper and the visiting nurses."

"Of course it's not for me."

Sebastian rummaged in a shopping bag and threw him a chocolate Santa Claus. Herr Schmidt didn't even consider trying to catch it. The smiling figure landed on the corner of the carpet.

"What are you crying for this time?"

"The question is, Father, why aren't *you* crying?"

Herr Schmidt went to his knees, slowly, so his joints didn't crack too loudly, reached for the chocolate Santa, and stood back up again. He waved Henry over, who was still waiting in the foyer by the coat closet.

"Why don't I cry? I'm not a little girl."

"Nor am I," sniffled Sebastian.

"Course you are. Come on, Henry. Let's open it." Bad enough that the boy had to see his father like this. Herr Schmidt sat down with Henry on the sofa in front of the television. They took turns breaking off pieces of the Santa as the chocolate melted in their fingers. Herr Schmidt's hands were soon all brown, though you could barely see it on Henry, of course.

"Do you go to church on Christmas," asked the boy with a full mouth.

"No."

"We do."

"I used to, Christmas Eve, because of Barbara. Never understood the point. This year she can't go, so we'll go next year again."

"So you'll stay here with Oma?"

"Exactly."

"So we'll come here?"

"I don't think so."

"Papa said we'd all come."

"Don't you have anything better to do?"

"Don't know," said Henry. "Are you going to decorate the tree in the garden again?"

Herr Schmidt had planned to put a few ornaments in the pear tree anyway, in case Barbara looked out the window. "Definitely. Any other questions?"

Henry shook his head. Sebastian, too, seemed to avoid the topic of Christmas this time. And yet it still hung in the air. They were sitting next to each other in front of the TV and watching Medinski knead lebkuchen dough when Herr Schmidt lost his patience.

"Not Christmas Eve," he said suddenly to Sebastian. "You've always come over on the 26th."

"But this year . . ."

"We need quiet around here, too," said Herr Schmidt. "Is that so difficult to understand?"

"And you'll spend Christmas Eve doing a sudoku at Mama's bedside? Or alone in front of the television?"

"I can imagine worse."

* * *

"Walter!" someone yelled, shaking his shoulder, his head flew back and forth, his neck cracked uncomfortably. He shoved the unfamiliar hand away and opened his eyes. He was sitting in his car, Hanne was leaning in the open driver's side door so that one of the buttons of her shirt was nearly touching his nose. He didn't know where he was or how he'd gotten there.

"Are you sleeping? Are you sick?"

He certainly wasn't well. Everything was dim, Hanne grew blurry for a moment, became clearly recognizable, then faded out once again. He took deep breaths.

"Where were you going?"

The car was at the gas station, two roundabouts from his home. It was shortly after nine, he couldn't remember what day, probably not a Thursday. Had he spent the night in the car?

"What are you doing here?" he snapped at Hanne once he was halfway conscious.

"Wanted to get a pack of cigarettes. The guy at the register asked if I knew the old guy outside, you've apparently been here for half an hour."

Half an hour, that wasn't so bad.

"Shall I drive you home?"

"You drive me? Ridiculous."

"Would you prefer to go straight to the doctor's?"

"Don't talk nonsense, dear girl."

Hanne walked around the car and got into the passenger's seat only to have to pull a bunch of parsley from under her bottom. She leaned forward, felt his forehead with her hand, pulled out a tissue, and wiped his face.

"You're bathed in sweat."

I'm scared, thought Herr Schmidt, but didn't say so. Otherwise Hanne would answer that she "understood," which would be a lie, because she would never understand. Not her, and not anyone else. He snatched the tissue from her and wiped his nose. She showed no sign of getting out.

"You going to sit here forever now?"

"What, you got someplace to be?"

"Yes," he said. "Artur's. I promised Barbara." Perhaps, he thought, she might even have heard him promise in her comatose state.

Hanne gulped. "And her?"

"Heike's there and the visiting nurse is coming later."

"You want to go alone?"

He didn't understand the question. He was always alone, did everything alone, up to now it had never been a problem.

"You've never been there," said Hanne.

"How do you know that?"

"Walter. Everyone knows that."

He cursed, started the engine. Had he at least filled the tank before he so oddly passed out? No, apparently he hadn't. Right, nozzle in, pay the guy at the register who'd sold Hanne her cigarettes and who looked at him now both nervously and relieved. Herr Schmidt's gaze fell on the shelf of chocolates, he took one, then another.

Back in the car he tossed one of the chocolate bars into Hanne's lap. She turned it around in her fingers and then put it in her pocket. He drove off, and in two minutes they were at the Golden Stag. But she showed no sign of getting out.

"No? Where should I drive you?"

"You can't go there alone. Not now, not like this, for the first time. I'll go with you."

Nonsense, he wanted to say, what if Barbara found out.

"We won't tell anyone," said Hanne, as if she were reading his thoughts, "it'll stay a secret." A secret with Hanne. It was so long ago. He threw his head back and laughed, the first time in years.

The good thing about her was that she didn't talk. She looked out the window, snoozed, ate her chocolate bar at some stage. She didn't ask about the route, as if she already knew exactly where they were going and how long it would take. Maybe she really did know everything, along with everyone else. Yeah, maybe he was the only one who believed things could disappear if you looked away for long enough.

At some point Hanne began to fidget with the wrapper of the chocolate bar, until he reached over and took it away from her. He didn't want to throw it out the window, so he balled it up and stuck it in his chest pocket.

The navigation device had calculated a drive time of two hours and 42 minutes. At least the unexpectedly long gas station episode had allowed him to miss rush hour on the autobahn. Before they turned off at the exit, he asked Hanne if she needed to use the bathroom. She said no. After they'd driven three quarters of an hour on the back road, he couldn't help thinking of how Barbara had always packed sandwiches for him if he had to go somewhere for work that was far enough to keep him from coming home for lunch. The thermos full of sweet, milky coffee had been small and heavy. His stomach tightened, what he wouldn't have given for a sip of that now.

"There's a bottle of water in the backseat," he said to Hanne. She twisted around, found the bottle, and gave it to him. Barbara would have opened it first. But it was no problem to screw open the cap while driving. He handed it back to Hanne, who took a drink from it without asking permission.

When first the name of the town and then the name of the institution appeared on street signs, Herr Schmidt began to tremble. He didn't understand where the sensation suddenly came from: freezer burn seemed to be eating its way through his guts like in a TV ad for freezer bags. He had imagined everything completely differently. The parking lot was half full. The windows of the institution were decorated like the kindergarten where Sebastian and Karin had gone years ago. It all looked so harmless, like a trap.

Hanne put her hand on his fingers, which were rattling on the steering wheel. His nails looked blue. Her warmth calmed him a bit. At some point it became embarrassing, so he got out. Hanne linked arms with him and pulled him to the entrance. The glass doors slid open silently, a few chairs stood in the vestibule. He had expected a waiting room like at a doctor's office, nurses who checked ID before they waved visitors through. Nothing like that. Hanne's hand still rested in the crook of his arm. He shook her off: what if the boy saw them like that? On the other hand, he probably had no idea who Herr Schmidt even was. How long ago was it that he'd last seen him?

"Where to now?" he whispered helplessly.

"You don't know where his room is?" asked Hanne. Obviously people didn't know everything about him after all.

She kept walking, across a burgundy carpet that Herr Schmidt might have expected in a hotel, not in an institution like this. He followed her. Hanne read the signs on the doors, knocked on one, and stuck her head inside.

"We were trying to visit Artur Schmidt . . . second floor, room 23? Thanks. Ah right, it's lunchtime? Thanks again." She turned to Herr Schmidt: "They're having lunch right now."

"We can wait in the car in the meantime," he mumbled, but then a woman with a round, friendly face appeared at the door and asked if they'd perhaps like to join for lunch. Herr Schmidt wasn't going to get out of this now. The woman led them down the hall and made several turns. Finally they went down a ramp and they were standing in front of the cafeteria. Hanne took Herr Schmidt's arm again, as if she sensed he would run away otherwise. The round-faced woman opened the glass doors with a fluid hand gesture and waved them in behind her. Herr Schmidt tried not to look to the left and right. He didn't know the place was more of a nursing home than a home for the disabled. Everywhere he saw aged people, far older than he and Hanne, with canes, in wheelchairs, younger people were few and far between. Artur was one of them, spooning up rice pudding opposite an old woman with white fuzz on her head. Herr Schmidt had recognized him right away, the shape of his head, his scrawny back, the drooping shoulders. He stopped cold, as if he'd taken root, removing himself from Hanne's grip.

"I can't. He doesn't even know me."

"He has a big picture of you hanging above his bed," said the woman, who was still at their side, as if she had no other work to take care of. "How is your wife, Herr Schmidt? I'm so sorry."

Herr Schmidt stared at Artur. He had made a mistake. It

came from losing your sense of time. Artur might have been one of the younger ones here, but he was certainly no longer young. He had graying hair, a creased face, and very light eyes, eyes that now noticed Hanne and apparently took a shine to her.

"Look who's here," said the nurse in a gentle singsong voice to Artur.

They sat down. There were exactly two empty chairs. Perhaps the people who usually occupied them had just died. The old woman sitting opposite Artur seemed afraid of Herr Schmidt and Hanne, but didn't move an inch to either side. She was actually blocking two spots. Herr Schmidt sat next to Artur, Hanne opposite him, pushed up against the woman next to her. He had no idea what to say, he was so horrified, like on the first day, and wanted to leave immediately. And what did Hanne do? She reached out her hand to Artur, said her name, gestured to Herr Schmidt, and said something about a car and the street. Artur strafed him with his gaze. Where had Herr Schmidt seen these light, nearly white eyes? Barbara's eyes had a different blue.

Then it hit him: in the mirror.

Artur couldn't really talk. He blurted out individual syllables excitedly, Hanne patted his hand. The old woman finally shifted over. Somebody came and brought Herr Schmidt a cup of coffee. Everyone knew who he was and who he belonged to. Rice pudding clung to the corners of Artur's mouth, Hanne picked up a napkin and wiped his face.

Toys, thought Herr Schmidt. Barbara had always bought toys. They always piled up in the basement before the holidays. She had liked to plan ahead. He reached into his jacket pocket, pulled out his chocolate bar, and handed it to Artur. In the corner of the cafeteria a Christmas tree blinked, a kitchen staffer cleared tables. The wheelchairs and canes had departed.

"Feel free to stay at the table," said a woman in a white cap who was wiping down a nearby table. "Look how happy he is."

Artur wasn't happy at all, at least not about Herr Schmidt. He was flirting with Hanne, who reached into her bag and pulled out a slightly dented chocolate surprise egg. Artur beamed and crushed it right away. They shared the chocolate and began to assemble the little toy inside. Herr Schmidt stood up and staggered into the hallway. He was afraid he was going to throw up in front of everyone.

On the way back Hanne drove. Barbara would never have managed that. How could he have expected that Hanne would be silent on the ride home, too? She talked nonstop. It slowly grew dark, the time went by quickly. The last thing they'd done was to sit in a room full of balls and toys and sculpt worms and eggs out of playdough. Artur had shown them his favorite car. They'd even taken a stroll in the wintry garden after they'd all bundled up appropriately. Artur's scarf had loosened during the walk so that the end trailed along the ground. Herr Schmidt had worried that the boy would step on it and strangle himself.

He remembered how much he used to worry about Karin and Sebastian when they were little. He had refused to go to the playground with them. Women's work, he had said. In reality, though, he died of fear at the thought alone, and it didn't stop until they were older and he found relief in the feeling that they were no longer the most vulnerable, painful part of his life.

"When do you want to tell him?" Hanne asked him on the autobahn.

"What?" Herr Schmidt snapped at her. Artur's uncomprehending "Mama?" still rang in his ears. "Leave me alone, Hanne."

They stopped at a rest stop and sat down at a table. Hanne got two cups of coffee, a piece of cheesecake, and two forks. Herr Schmidt looked at his hands, they were no longer trembling, that had stopped at some stage.

"How old is Artur? A bit older than Bernd, right?"

He knew she was cruel. He had been thinking the same thing the whole time and wondered when she would say it.

"I don't know how old Bernd is," he lied.

"I can't understand how Barbara could forgive you for never visiting him," said Hanne offhandedly.

Herr Schmidt's stiff fingers battled with the tiny packet of coffee creamer. "She didn't. She's hated me ever since. Never stopped."

"That's ridiculous. You were a good couple." Hanne froze, then corrected herself: "You are a good couple."

"Nonsense. You know it yourself. There's no such thing as a good couple if I'm part of it."

Hanne shrugged her shoulders and looked out the window.

"You got lucky back then," he said. "That nothing came of it."

"No doubt." She took the creamer from him and ripped it open without spilling a single drop. Typical barkeeper.

"I was young, it was just a laugh. I didn't even want to marry her. My mother was opposed to it. We had only just escaped the Russians, and if we're being honest, Barbara was one of them in those days. But then there was a child on the way." The fact that he could say all of this, without being struck by lightning—and to Hanne of all people, who exploited every weakness, who didn't let anyone get away with anything. He knew he would bitterly regret it. "In those days nobody could tell in advance what a baby was going to be like. What was I supposed to do? She cried so much."

"Walter. Everybody knows this." Hanne put her warm fingers on his ice-cold hand.

He did not pull it away.

He had dropped Hanne off at the Golden Stag, headed home, and sent Heike, who was sitting next to Barbara reading a comic book, on her way. He sat down on the edge of the bed and turned so he would see the same thing as Barbara if she were to open her eyes, the dark sky framed by wild grape vines. Then he closed the curtains and put on the lamp on the nightstand. Barbara's eyelids fluttered. Then he sat down on the prewarmed chair next to the bed and took Barbara's hand.

"I was there," he said.

Barbara seemed to be listening attentively.

"He's a big guy, and he's gotten old. None of us is getting any younger." He leaned back, closed his eyes, in his mind he pictured Hanne picking up the cheesecake. It used to be his favorite kind of cake. His thoughts raced and in the end were overwhelmed by images he had long banned from his head. Barbara never wanted to give Artur up, but it still played out that way. He had wanted other, regular children. "You'd never have managed it otherwise," he said. "I know you hate me, but what else could I have done back then. Tell me, Barbara!" The sentences poured out of him. He was no longer so sure she was really listening. From that point on, Herr Schmidt just went on thinking, without speaking. That was another way of conversing, after all: silently, in thoughts. You didn't have him under control. You didn't have any kind of life anymore. I was no help to you. Children are women's work. I had to keep us fed. And I was right—Sebastian and Karin only came along after he was gone. I'd promised to take care of you, and I kept my word. What I'm doing now is part of that, too. I don't mean the cooking, I mean everything else, the things we've never discussed. I could have done other things—but instead I'm doing it the way you want. Do you think it's easy? Nothing's ever easy. I wouldn't have hit him. I never hit you, either. Or did I?

He was still lost in thought when suddenly his head started to buzz. The words disappeared, yielded to images that suddenly surrounded him: Herr Schmidt's birthday, how young they still are, and how old they feel. Barbara's bouffant hairdo, despite Artur she still manages to make herself look beautiful. Freshly-baked cheesecake on the table, she'd finally mastered it. Herr Schmidt's mother would be by soon for coffee and birthday cake, though she'd bring her own cake. She's afraid Barbara will poison her. He's putting on a clean shirt when he hears the noise in the living room. He immediately feels sick to his stomach, which is his default sensation at the time. When he reaches the doorway he sees the boy clawing with both hands at the cake and stuffing it into his mouth. At the sight of Herr Schmidt he initially laughs, then starts to cry. Herr Schmidt doesn't hit him, the boy cries anyway, cowering against the wall. I will kill you—but they're only words.

* * *

"Who's the woman who always calls here," Sebastian asked as they were sitting together on the second Sunday of advent.

"I don't know any woman."

"Has some kind of accent."

"Oh, her. Nut case."

"She sounds nice." Sebastian lit two of the candles that Karin had put on the table the previous weekend.

"Women."

"How do you know her?"

"Through Medinski," grumbled Herr Schmidt. He was angry at Lydia for compromising him to such an extent that his family now must think badly of him. Meaning, more badly than normal. Hopefully Sebastian hasn't told Barbara. "She has two tickets for Medinski's event and doesn't want to go alone."

"Go with her," said Sebastian, picking at the candle wax.

"I don't want to upset your mother. She'll get the wrong idea."

Sebastian pulled quite a lot of wax off the candle before he answered. "I honestly don't believe she'll get the wrong idea."

"You don't know your mother."

"Father. You've been sitting around here for ages, you only go out to shop. Go see Medinski. It'll do you good."

"Nonsense," snarled Herr Schmidt. Sebastian had no idea. He didn't know anything about the excursion with Hanne or anything else.

"Is she nice?" asked Sebastian. "The one who always calls?"

"She's a pest. What are you smiling at."

* * *

His pear preserves had come out well: better than the store-bought ones and nicer looking than the pictures on the internet. He had experimented with different mixtures of sugar and cooking times. He turned over the jars, which he had placed upside down after filling. The preserves had the perfect consistency, slid down the side of the jar at just the right speed, not too runny, not too solid. If you held the jar up to the light, golden bits of fruit shimmered. Heike had brought him labels. He wrote "Pear" along with the year on seven of them, stuck them to the jars, and looked at the time. Medinski's appearance was to start in fifteen minutes. Herr Schmidt wanted to sit down in front of the television, but Sebastian had dozed off on the sofa. He should go ahead and relax, a bit of sleep would do him good. Herr Schmidt was about to close the door to the room when Sebastian awoke with a start. "What's up with Mama?"

"Sleeping," said Herr Schmidt. "You should, too."

Sebastian stretched out again, his eyes gleamed in the dark.

"Do you think," mumbled Herr Schmidt, "it would be bad if I went to see Medinski now?" He hoped Sebastian wouldn't even hear him. But he raised a thumbs-up from his lying-down position.

He reached the city in twenty minutes. Finding the specific

place took much longer. He had been proud of his sense of orientation in the past, and resisted using a navigation system. But now he was short on time. He capitulated and turned the thing on, just to make sure he was in the right area. It was a neighborhood of villas with huge yards, cobblestone streets, nothing he hadn't seen during his former working days. There'd been a time when he installed appliances in houses that other people only ever saw on TV: high ceilings, parquet floors, ugly vases. Coffee in tiny cups, and always much too strong. The people were always friendly, grateful for quality work. But you had to ask for milk and sugar.

Herr Schmidt parked in a side street and went on foot to the event space, which because of the name he had initially taken for a restaurant but which turned out to be a strange hybrid of bookstore, café, and kitchen utensil shop. Herr Schmidt was uncomfortable turning up late. He was therefore prepared to pay the full price for the ticket, no matter how horrendous the cost. But the woman sitting at the entrance with a lockable metal cash drawer full of coins refused to let him in: "Sold out."

Herr Schmidt wasn't daunted by this nonsense, put his money on the table, pushed the woman, who had now stood up, out of the way, causing an unnecessary uproar.

"It's okay! We're together!" Lydia was suddenly there, with red eyes and her scarf askew. The woman at the entrance breathed excitedly, shook her head disapprovingly. "It was a misunderstanding." Lydia smiled at her, linked elbows with Herr Schmidt, and towed him into a sort of giant kitchen, where rows of chairs stood. Leaning against the counter was the real-life Medinski, an open book in his hand. People turned toward Herr Schmidt. Medinski kept reading, undisturbed. Herr Schmidt sat down on a chair from which Lydia removed her handbag. He unbuttoned his coat, and the top of his shirt as well. So many people, so little oxygen. Lydia beamed at him from the side. He tried to follow Medinski. It was something about his grandmother and childhood. Herr Schmidt rubbed his face and tried to shield himself from Lydia's attention, which tortured him as much as a space heater sitting too close to him. He had always avoided sitting around with groups of people. Now he realized once again why.

At some point Lydia rammed her elbow into his side. "Walter! You can't be serious!"

He opened his eyes. The rows of seats were empty. "What happened?"

"At first I thought you were still listening! You didn't really sleep through the whole show, did you?"

"Where's Medinski?"

"Signing books." Lydia gestured over her shoulder.

"Then I can leave."

"I want him to sign a book for me."

"What book?"

"The one he read from. The one you're about to buy for me."

Barbara would never have been so brazen. Herr Schmidt opted not to engage in a discussion, pulled out his wallet, and gave Lydia a twenty euro note. "Buy it yourself. How much do I owe you for the ticket?"

"Ach, Walter. I won them in the contest."

She left him standing there and joined the long line. Herr Schmidt waited. Then he went a few steps closer and glimpsed Medinski at the head of the line, framed by several piles of books. The woman who hadn't wanted to let in Herr Schmidt took money, picked up books from the piles, unwrapped them, and opened them to the correct page. The customers leaned down and spoke to Medinksi. Herr Schmidt could see from this distance what apparently escaped all the people standing directly in front of him: Medinski had no desire for chitchat, was tired, and wanted to go home. The line slowly dwindled. Lydia was second to last. He wondered if he should just leave and drive home. Then he realized that would be cowardly. He stood there rooted and waited while she bought her book, just as he had waited countless times for Barbara when she went shopping, chatted with people, or looked for a public restroom, as if they didn't have one at home.

Medinski wiped his brow with a cloth handkerchief. Herr Schmidt's legs were falling asleep. He set himself in motion, walking along the shelves displaying simple pots and baking forms that cost as much as quality power tools. He'd already made his way well into the unlit part of the space when Lydia called his name. "Ready," she said, triumphantly brandishing the book, the cover of which featured Medinski framed by an assortment of off-putting vegetables.

The nervous woman who hadn't wanted to let Herr Schmidt enter was already packing the leftover books into boxes. Medinski stood next to her, wrapping a scarf around his neck. Herr Schmidt walked past him: he had pictured the chef taller and much fatter. As he and Lydia, who had once again linked elbows with him, approached the automatic sliding doors, he remembered. He turned around and went up to Medinski, who peered at him with a look of slight concern.

"I totally forgot." Herr Schmidt fished in his coat pocket and pulled out a jar of preserves. "For you."

Medinski finished looping his scarf and took the jar in both hands. "That's terribly kind of you."

"We spoke about it. On the internet."

"Did we?" Medinski studied the label, held the jar up to the light. "Aha. Pears?"

"From my garden."

"And you are?"

"Schmidt, Walter." Herr Schmidt put out his hand. Medinski shook it firmly like a real man.

"And this is your wife?" Medinski nodded toward Lydia.

"No. I don't actually know her. My wife is Barbara."

Medinski looked as if he were trying to remember something.

"So, auf Wiedersehen." Herr Schmidt now took Lydia's elbow and pulled her away. At the door he whispered to her: "Why didn't you give away the second ticket to somebody else? I said I couldn't make it."

"Ach, Walter." Lydia squeezed his hand. "I knew you'd come."

Lydia had taken public transport there, so now, of course, he had to drive her home. She filled the car with her perfume, and he immediately wondered what Barbara would say about it. She was so sensitive to smells. Hanne had, as usual, reeked of cigarettes during their drive, though it had only registered later. At which point he had driven around with the windows open and nearly caught a cold as a result.

"What was it you gave to him?" asked Lydia as she erratically directed him toward her home. Instead of saying which direction to go, she waved her hands around and yelled at the last second: "Here! Here! Ach, Walter!"

"Who did I give something to?"

"Medinski."

"Nothing." He figured she'd want a jar, as well, but didn't want to give her one. He was stingy and proud of it.

"So how's Barbara?"

"Better."

"What are you doing for Christmas?"

"We'll be home. The children are coming."

Now it was his turn to ask her something, what she was doing, for instance. But he didn't want to know. He realized he was being impolite, more impolite than usual, but he could barely stand to be alone with her in the car. The fact that he wasn't shouting at her was already more than you could demand of him. When they came to a halt in a parking lot in front of a high-rise not far from the autobahn, he was surprised.

"This is where you live?"

"Why?"

He had often driven past and every time had wondered how anyone could live in the place, the small apartments with no yards, full of foreigners. Even if you were one.

"Shall I take you upstairs?"

Lydia's eyes lit up.

"Not like that," he said gruffly. "To the door of the apartment. I shudder to think of all those who might be hanging around those halls."

"I'm an old woman, what could happen to me?" Lydia smiled coquettishly.

"Right," said Herr Schmidt. "Then I'll be off. Barbara's waiting."

Her smile disappeared, she finally got out. She left Medinski's book sitting there.

"Hey, Lydia, your book."

"It's for you."

"Why?" he shouted out the open window, as she had already moved away from the car. "Why all of this, Lydia? Is every other man dead already?"

"Yep. And because you're so handsome."

Before he could protest, she had disappeared into the dark.

* * *

Christmas Eve passed nearly unnoticed. Herr Schmidt had considered making Medinski's warm potato salad, but then hadn't felt like doing all the cutting and peeling. Barbara didn't care for potato salad anyway, she used to make it once in a while for Herr Schmidt's sake, though it never came out so great. Herr Schmidt tossed a couple bratwurst into a pan and sat down in front of the television. Later he looked in on Barbara, wiped the cake crumbs from her chin, and took Helmut out.

It was dark, windows and front yards were lit up, the streets were devoid of people. Why had it never occurred to him how beautiful Christmas Eve could be? What had they usually done on this day? Barbara went to a long church service, afterwards they ate and watched TV. Gifts would have been silly, they had everything. Even so, there had always been a sense of unease, as if something was supposed to happen. But today everything was just right.

His feet had carried him across the market square. He walked through the little copse of trees, past the apartment block where Heike lived. She had off, though she hadn't asked for it off; still, he wasn't inhuman, he had forbidden her to come on the holidays. Herr Schmidt studied her doorbell, the lone German name must have been hers, he knew only her first name, didn't need to know more. All the rest of the residents were Yugoslavs and Turks, though some of the windows were decorated anyway. He leaned his head back until his neck hurt.

A few hundred meters beyond, bells began to ring, suddenly attracting his attention. He arrived at just the right moment to see a throng of people stream out of the church, a laughing, festive bunch, old people, couples, a few older children—people with little children must have been at the earlier family service. He thought he recognized Hanne's shock of hair in the middle of the throng. The mountain of a man next to her was probably Bernd, who with his gray hair looked older than his mother from behind. Herr Schmidt turned around abruptly, would be just his luck if they spotted him. Before the stupid dog could draw attention to them by howling with joy, he tightened his leash and pulled him along behind him into a side street. In the underpass by the train station the homeless person sat next to a dog, which, as always, looked dead. Herr Schmidt yanked the leash before Helmut could try to grab something from the bags stuffed with food.

"Happy New Year," the homeless person mumbled as they went past.

* * *

Herr Schmidt had already suspected Barbara would have no interest in the wild boar goulash. It seemed as if she didn't even want to hear him describe the color and consistency of it. She could go ahead and stick with her cakes, like a little child, the important thing was that she ate. He didn't want to put too much effort into the meal when it was just for him, so the red cabbage came from a can, the spätzle from the refrigerator section.

Karin called just as he was warming up the cabbage in a saucepan.

"Papa, your preserves were on TV."

"What are you taking about?"

"Really. Medinski showed the jar on camera for at least a minute and philosophized about it."

"Passed it off as his own?"

"Not at all. Said it was a gift from a stranger."

"I'll go look. Taking the phone with me."

"The show's already over. You'll have to click the hamburger icon and find the video archive."

"Speak German to me."

"Wait a sec, I'll send you a link."

On the telephone table, the mobile with the big screen that Sebastian had recently left for him chirped. Herr Schmidt couldn't and didn't want to start using it.

He heaped food onto a plate and carried it upstairs to the bedroom. Sat down on the chair next to Barbara. "Couple of snowflakes would be nice, eh?" he asked. He had a feeling he was disturbing her with his chomping. The red cabbage wasn't thoroughly heated, he left quite a lot of it, put the plate on the windowsill, stroked Barbara's hair.

Back down in the kitchen, he pulled out a large Tupperware container and slopped in the rest of the food from the pot, which turned out to be a mistake, because the result was an unappetizing mound. He should have used three smaller containers. He wrapped several slices of fruitcake in foil and put it all in the basket Barbara had used to shop in the old days. "Too bad," he said to Helmut's expectant face. "Not this time."

He was worried the homeless person would no longer be in the underpass. Part of him even hoped that was the case. But of course the person was still there, where else. Herr Schmidt got down on his knees with a groan and began to unpack what he had brought onto a dishtowel he spread out.

"What's this?" asked the homeless person, without any particular delight.

"Christmas," said Herr Schmidt. "The red cabbage is from a can, but I reheated it." Barbara's sweater, in which he had wrapped everything, had kept everything surprisingly warm. He handed the person the open Tupperware container and took a fork from a napkin. The homeless person took the fork tentatively, speared a piece of goulash, and sniffed it.

"Lamb?"

"Wild boar."

The person nodded appreciatively, taking a first bite and starting to chew. Herr Schmidt watched for a moment, thought better of it, and shifted his gaze elsewhere. The person had so many bags, why the need for so much stuff? Kneeling was no longer viable, the cold of the concrete seeped through Herr Schmidt's workpants directly into his joints. Still, any other position would have been even more uncomfortable. With a grunt he shoved Barbara's sweater under his knees.

"Want some?" asked the homeless person.

Herr Schmidt waved his hand. "Already ate."

Up close you could now see that the homeless person was

definitely a man. The heavy jaw, thick neck. Strands of hair fell down over his face, he wiped his mouth with his sleeve, even though Herr Schmidt had purposefully brought napkins. The little dog finally awoke and watched the movement of the man's jaw as if hypnotized. Herr Schmidt fished around in his jacket pocket, there were always a couple of dog treats.

The man had emptied the container in no time and unwrapped the fruitcake from the foil. "Your wife bake this?"

"No, I did."

"Got no wife?"

"I do," said Herr Schmidt. "Barbara. Not too healthy at the moment. Not too tall, thin. Blue eyes, wears a light-brown jacket. Looks younger than she is. Handsome woman."

"I know her."

"Right."

"No, really. From the YCC."

"Does everybody know Barbara?"

The homeless man shrugged his shoulders. The fruitcake was gone, all three slices.

"Full?" asked Herr Schmidt.

The guy shook his head.

"Always the same with you guys." Herr Schmidt tried to stand back up, but it took a few attempts. The homeless man, only half Herr Schmidt's age, probably took some spiteful glee at the sight.

Herr Schmidt felt anger welling up inside himself. "Why do you sit here anyway? Why don't you work? Are you sick? Are you incapacitated?" He didn't expect an answer, not even a thank you. He had to bend down to start gathering his things into the basket, the sweater on top. "If you have healthy arms and legs, you have to work," he said tartly. "Don't want to embarrass yourself in front of your dog."

The man said nothing, his eyes fixed on the ground. Herr Schmidt had finally finished rounding everything up. It annoyed him that the man didn't even defend himself. Herr Schmidt waited for something to happen. He had hoped for a different, liberating feeling. Instead the icy cold became more unbearable with every passing second, and he had to restrain himself to keep from kicking all the stuffed plastic bags.

* * *

The morning of the second day of Christmas he had no desire left to cook. "You don't eat anything anyway," he told Barbara, whose fluttering eyelids seemed to prove his point. He sat down at the computer and marveled at the photo of Medinski holding up his, that is Herr Schmidt's, pear preserves to the camera, staying out of the discussion as to whether it would become *the* jam the following fall and how people could get the secret recipe. Medinski had apparently speculated about the ratio of regular sugar to jelly sugar and also vowed to test various mixtures as soon as decent pears were available again. Go ahead, thought Herr Schmidt indifferently. His pear tree stood there bare and looked dead once again despite the ornaments and tinsel Herr Schmidt had hung from it. Beneath a post asking for the best recipes for Christmas leftovers, he considered writing that he didn't feel like cooking anymore. That cooking was actually the most useless task in the world. You put in effort, wasted time, and in the end everything was either consumed or went bad and was thrown out. Whether you cooked well or not, whether you cooked at all, it didn't change anything in the grand scheme of life. He held his fingers above the keyboard, intending to write out this insight, when he thought of Lydia. What would it be like for her to read something like that? He left the computer, still on. Maybe he should call her. Not that she was sitting alone, waiting by the phone.

* * *

Just when he thought he had survived the holidays, the children arrived. Karin and Mai came first, they'd spent part of the holidays with Mai's family in southern Germany. They entered the foyer quietly, as if someone might be sleeping, then they wandered through the house and found Herr Schmidt sitting in front of the television, which was turned off, slumped with his head propped on his hands, napping.

"Papa?" Karin staggered over to him and began to feel his neck. "What's wrong, Papa?"

He shoved her away. "What would be wrong with me?"

"Such a beautiful tree, Walter!" said Mai with her face pressed to the window, which would no doubt leave greasy marks behind.

"Just a normal old tree."

They were both quiet by their standards, moved subtly, barely talked. Some bag was unpacked in the kitchen. He still just sat there. Heard Sebastian arrive. Couldn't hear whether the boy was with him. Herr Schmidt didn't stir.

"Father." Sebastian stuck his head in the door. "Merry Christmas."

"Same to you."

"Why are the gifts for the visiting nurses still on the windowsill?"

"No idea." He had completely forgotten about them, and instead had given each of them a fifty euro note and a chocolate Santa.

Sebastian looked as if he wanted to say something, but then changed his mind. "Henry, do you want to say hello to Opa?" Herr Schmidt heard. "Why not? That's impolite."

I don't want to say hello to anyone, either, thought Herr Schmidt.

Now Karin again. "Papa, am I disturbing you?"

"Yes."

"Sorry, I just wanted to ask, so there aren't any misunderstandings. What do you have planned for dinner tonight?"

"Nothing."

"What?"

"What about *nothing* is unclear?"

Karin blinked. "That's something of a surprise. We didn't prepare anything because we assumed you would have planned everything, like always. We didn't want to meddle, you dislike that so much. Is there anything in the freezer?"

"How should I know?"

Karin disappeared, Mai came in a moment later and brought him a cup of something that smelled like a urinal cake. "Herbal tea okay with you?"

"Sure," said Herr Schmidt just to get rid of her.

"Walter, we were thinking, it's a bit unconventional, of course, but perhaps we could all take our plates up to the bedroom so we can be with Barbara, what do you think? I'm sure she would sense our presence somehow. Does that work for you?" When he didn't react, she patted him on the shoulder. "Thanks!" If they wanted to eat in the bedroom and shower in the TV room then, please, they should be his guests, thought Herr Schmidt dully. It was Christmas.

He didn't say goodbye to anyone, not even Barbara. They were all suddenly busy fussing over preparations for dinner anyway, as if they'd been starving for days, gathering leftovers and pantry staples, pulling something out of the freezer. It was perfect for Herr Schmidt. He crept out, though Helmut nearly gave him away. "You can't come," Herr Schmidt had hissed at him. "You keep an eye on things here." He sat down at the wheel, saw the windows of his own house lit up in the rearview mirror, and stepped on the gas like he was being chased. He didn't need the navigation system, could still remember the way well. The route was simple: autobahn, then from the off-ramp follow the signs. Pitiful little drops fell from the sky. Winters used to be snowy, thought Herr Schmidt. But other than that, nothing had been better back then.

He drove into the parking lot, which was much emptier than the first time. Holiday staffing, thought Herr Schmidt. The entire building seemed abandoned. Most of the people were probably with their families. This time he had to find his way without Hanne. A few things were totally new: the sweet smell hadn't registered during the first visit, nor had all the stairs and the strange paintings on the walls.

A woman approached him, and he couldn't tell whether she worked there, lived there, or was visiting. He grabbed her sleeve and asked for Artur. She knew Artur and helped him look.

Artur sat in one of the common rooms pushing toy cars around on a carpet printed with streets. He made humming noises in various tones as he played. Herr Schmidt stopped in the doorway. He realized with surprise that Artur had a pretty good idea of how intersections and traffic lights worked. That hadn't been true when he was a little boy.

"It's me," said Herr Schmidt, going to his knees as he had recently on the concrete, and his joints remembered more quickly than his head. "Do you remember me?"

Artur mumbled something that sounded like "Mama."

"Alas, young man," mumbled Herr Schmidt in response. He reached his hand out to Artur. Artur got up with astonishing ease and helped Herr Schmidt to his feet with a strange laugh. Strong, thought Herr Schmidt approvingly. He's stronger than I am now.

Later, at the wheel, he decided he'd done everything wrong. He had just taken Artur, without signing him out and without taking any luggage. Maybe there was a stuffed animal or something the boy absolutely needed for the night. Sebastian had needed his teddy bear until he was fourteen.

"They'll probably think I've kidnapped you." Herr Schmidt looked into Artur's eyes in the rearview mirror. The boy seemed apprehensive, scared. "You think so, too?"

The first few minutes of the drive went smoothly. But at some stage Artur began to make strange, question-like noises. Herr Schmidt tried to explain things to him, but it didn't help, so he turned on the radio. That worked surprisingly well. As they drove down the autobahn Artur was thrilled by the speed.

"Have you never done this? Only Sunday drivers out here right now. Come on, we'll go a little faster. Normally there's a lot of traffic."

The little droplets left smudges on the windshield. He hadn't even dressed the boy properly. Maybe he was freezing. Herr Schmidt was always bad about that sort of stuff, forgot a scarf here, left a hat there. Once he forgot Artur himself on a park bench, where had Barbara been anyway? The boy was gone, the entire town went out looking for him. Herr Schmidt hadn't understood why Barbara had been so distraught.

He had a feeling he had to explain everything to Artur. But perhaps Artur understood a thing or two. Herr Schmidt hadn't even brought a Christmas present—such a thing had never occurred to him before. He could have pressed money into his hand, like the girls from the visiting nurse service, after all they needed money more desperately than Sebastian's daintily wrapped herbal teas. But what would the boy do with money? Surely he wasn't allowed to go shopping on his own.

"Do you need to go?" Herr Schmidt had remembered that children constantly needed to use the bathroom. How upset he used to get with Karin and Sebastian and their requests to stop. Which of them had gone in their pants that time while driving in the mountains because Herr Schmidt hadn't wanted to pull over? Maybe it had been both of them.

He stopped at the same rest stop where he'd had a coffee with Hanne, opened the car door, and yanked Artur out. Artur screamed like an animal, Herr Schmidt tried to do it more gently. He took the boy's tense hand and entered the rest stop, immediately saw the table where he'd sat with Hanne, now occupied by a suspicious-looking old timer. There were simply no normal people out and about on this day. The few customers and the server stared.

"What?" asked Herr Schmidt. "Never seen a disabled person before?" He forgot why he was there, picked a table, and put Artur in a chair, but the boy stood right back up. "They have cheesecake here," said Herr Schmidt, but Artur got agitated, started making noises and didn't want to sit down at any cost. "What is it? No cheesecake?"

He had the impression that Artur was answering in the affirmative.

"Fine by me. We won't get cheesecake. I'll make you one at home."

He held Artur's hand firmly so he didn't bang the sugar dispenser on the table.

"In that case we'll just keep driving. They're all waiting already anyway."

Europa Editions UK

Read the World

Literary fiction, popular fiction, narrative non-fiction,
travel, memoir, world noir

Building bridges between cultures with the finest writing from around the world.

Ahmet Altan, Peter Cameron, Andrea Camilleri, Catherine Chidgey,
Sandrine Collette, Christelle Dabos, Donatella Di Pietrantonio, Négar Djavadi,
Deborah Eisenberg, Elena Ferrante, Lillian Fishman, Anna Gavalda,
Saleem Haddad, James Hannaham, Jean-Claude Izzo, Maki Kashimada,
Nicola Lagioia, Alexandra Lapierre, Grant Morrison, Ondjaki, Valérie Perrin,
Christopher Prendergast, Eric-Emmanuel Schmitt, Domenico Starnone,
Esther Yi, Charles Yu

Acts of Service, *Didn't Nobody Give a Shit What Happened to Carlotta*,
Ferocity, *Fifteen Wild Decembers*, *Fresh Water for Flowers*, *Lambda*,
Love in the Days of Rebellion, *My Brilliant Friend*, *Remote Sympathy*,
Sleeping Among Sheep Under a Starry Sky, *Total Chaos*, *Transparent City*,
What Happens at Night, *A Winter's Promise*

Europa Editions was founded by Sandro Ferri and Sandra Ozzola,
the owners of the Rome-based publishing house Edizioni E/O.

Europa Editions UK is an independent trade publisher
based in London.

www.europaeditions.co.uk

Follow us at . . .
Twitter: @EuropaEdUK
Instagram: @EuropaEditionsUK
TikTok: @EuropaEditionsUK